I0521377

Storylandia

The Wapshott Journal of Fiction

Issue 10

The Wapshott Press

Storylandia, Issue 10, The Wapshott Journal of Fiction, ISSN 1947-5349, ISBN 978-0-9848325-8-3, is published at intervals by the Wapshott Press, PO Box 31513, Los Angeles, California, 90031-0513, telephone 323-201-7147. All correspondence can be sent The Wapshott Press, PO Box 31513, LA CA 90031-0513. Visit our website at www.WapshottPress.com This work is copyright © 2013 by Storylandia. The Wapshott Journal of Fiction, Los Angeles, California. "Death Among the Marshes" is copyright © 2013 Kathryn L. Ramage and is reprinted here with the copyright owner's permission. Copyright for the cover artwork is held by the artist and is reprinted here with the copyright owner's permission.

Storylandia is always seeking quality original short stories, novelettes, and novellas. Please have a look at our submission guidelines at www.Storylandia. WapshottPress.com or email the editor at editor@wapshottpress.com

Many thanks to William Akin for the proofread and editorial support.

Cover: "Misty" by Eleanor Leonne Bennett, www.eleanorleonnebennett.com

Storylandia

The Wapshott Journal
of Fiction

Founded in 2009

Issue 10, Summer 2013

Edited by Ginger Mayerson

Table of Contents

Kathryn L. Ramage

Death Among the Marshes
A Murder Mystery Set in the Twenties

1

A lady in a heavy fur coat unsuitable for the warm, spring weather stood at the inner door of the train compartment, frowning at the two young men seated before her. One of these young men, Frederick Arthur Babington by name, assumed that her scowl was one of disapproval at the cigarette gripped between his nervous fingertips. A filthy habit to indulge indoors, but one that he'd picked up during the Great War and found soothing during troubled moments. Since he was currently traveling with his friend and manservant Billy Watkins to the Norfolk town of Downham Market and thereafter to Marsh Hall to attend the funeral of his cousin Bertram Marsh, this was certainly one of those troubled times.

Before he could offer to open the window, however, the lady made the true source of her displeasure known. "This is a First Class carriage," she announced, her eyes on Billy.

Billy shrank into his seat and looked as if he

might creep away to another section of the train more suitable for a working-class lad, but Freddie wasn't so easily intimidated. "We are quite aware of that, Madam," he responded. "I assure you that we both have the appropriate tickets."

"You keep your servant with you, young man?" she inquired with a scornful note.

"Everywhere I go," Freddie answered. "I couldn't get on without him."

The lady didn't find this an acceptable answer. "Is this what England is coming to?"

"I'm afraid so, Madam," said Freddie. "The war, you know, changed everything."

The woman huffed and went away down the corridor in search of a compartment where she wouldn't be exposed to the indiscriminate mixing of classes.

"You oughtn't've spoke to her that way," Billy said softly once they were alone. "'Tisn't respectful to a lady, even if she ain't respectful herself."

"Well, she bally well wasn't," Freddie responded with indignation, feeling the slight to his friend more acutely than his friend did himself. "What business of hers is it if we sit here together? Why shouldn't a decent and respectable young lad like yourself who served King and Country sit in a First-Class compartment if you like to and you have the money to pay for it?"

"It was your money what paid for it," Billy reminded his friend.

Freddie dismissed this point with a wave of his hand. "What does that matter? The ticket was paid for. You have as much right to sit here as my uncle Lord Marshbourne himself. We fought to make the world a better place, Billy my lad. If that means that ridiculous old-fashioned customs and rigid notions of class go out the window, so much the better! Victoria's been dead for over twenty years, and the Victorian age died with her. We've got a new and thoroughly modern age to face up to now."

Billy regarded his friend with a mix of admiration and misgiving. He wasn't sure that *he* was ready for this new age yet. Frederick Babington had been to university; he was certainly much more clever than Billy, but some of the things he said were alarming. Soshy, Billy's dad would call Freddie's kind of talk. But the grandson of a viscount could get away with soshy talk.

The two had known each other since they were boys. Billy's father had been manservant to the celebrated scholar Sir Hilliard Babington for over forty years. Billy, his brothers, and sisters had practically grown up in the back garden of the old gentleman's home near Cambridge, and he had first met Freddie when he'd come to visit his uncle during the holidays as a child. They'd become better acquainted when Freddie had come to study at Cambridge and to assist his uncle in compiling his memoirs for publication.

Freddie had been just a few weeks short of his 19th birthday in the summer of 1914 and at the end of his first year at Cambridge when the war began. Like any decent chap, Freddie had enlisted. Sir Hilliard had arranged for Billy, who also signed up a few weeks later, to be assigned as his nephew's batman.

"Freddie will look after you, my lad," Sir Hilliard had told Billy before seeing him off.

"You're too promising to be blown to bits on a battlefield."

No one had foreseen that, once they'd gone to the front, he would end up looking after Freddie. Hadn't he shot German soldiers—the only shots he'd ever fired during the war—when they'd tried to take Freddie prisoner? And hadn't he stood over his injured friend after a bomb had exploded over the company headquarters, keeping watch and weeping until the stretcher arrived?

He'd continued in Freddie's service since they'd been demobbed, taking care of the London flat while his friend was in hospital. Freddie's wounds had healed and his injured limbs were growing strong again, but his mind still needed time to recover. Billy knew that better than anyone else. He'd often been jolted awake in the middle of night by screams from the master bedroom at the far end of the flat.

The Great War had made many boys into old men, but in spite of all he'd suffered, Frederick Babington still looked surprisingly youthful for his 26 years. He was a pale, intense, and solemn young man—more pale, Billy thought, since he'd been wounded so terribly. At least he no longer limped and the burn scars on the small and ring fingers of his left hand were now only puckered reddish skin. His dark hair had been cropped short during his last stay in a private nursing home over the winter past, but it was growing out again and beginning to curl just as it used to.

Billy watched as one loose curl fell forward over Freddie's brow as he returned his attention to the book he'd been reading before the interruption, a newly published mystery novel titled *Whose*

Body? When Freddie lifted his eyes from the page a moment later, Billy pretended an interest in the book.

"What's that one about?"

"There's a dead body that turns up in a bathtub, quite starkers—not a stitch on except for a pair of gold *pince nez*—and nobody seems to know who the dead chap is, not even the people who live in the flat where the bathtub is."

"I don't see how you can read such things, about dead bodies and such, after- well- after seeing so many dead folk yourself in the trenches." Billy felt sure that dwelling on the subject of murder had done no good for Freddie's state of mind.

But Freddie responded, "This is different. It's not real, you know. The murders in these stories are always somewhat fantastic and never have the true stink and ugliness of death about them, not at all like the terrible things you and I have seen. And it's all cleaned up in the end. I'm quite certain the detective chap in this one will find out who the naked body in the bath is and discover who put him there in the last chapter. They always do. It's quite comforting in its way."

He set the book down across his knee. "All the same, Billy," he admitted, "I can't help noticing how the war's begun to creep in. I first started to read murder mysteries as a sort of escape into fiction. But in this one, the fellow who's doing the detecting has been through it just the same as we have. He's even been shell-shocked. The one I read before this, you remember, about that funny little Belgian detective? Well, *he* was a refugee and his sidekick was home on leave after being wounded. The war was all around the edges of that story. I think I prefer good old Sherlock Holmes to these modern mysteries. He's a touch old-fashioned, but the worst you'll find in those pages is poor Dr. Watson's wandering wound from some Afghan campaign. Nothing to remind me of things I'd rather forget."

They were within a few miles of the Downham Market rail station. As Freddie looked out at the familiar, flat countryside, he sighed.

"I could've come here when I was just out of hospital," he told Billy. "The family would've been glad to have me home again, but I couldn't do it. Marsh Hall is too noisy and crowded. Too full of well-meaning aunties who would make an endless fuss over me. Once I was through with the war, all I wanted to do was rest and read and try to pick up my life where I left it off in `14. I wouldn't have come here now if it weren't for Bertie's dying so suddenly."

"This cousin of yours," asked Billy. "Was you and him close?"

"We grew up together at Marsh Hall," Freddie answered. "He was my first half-cousin, just like Kell, but a year or so closer to my own age than Kell is."

"I never heard you mention him `til you got that telegram about his being drowned." Although the young Marshes had also visited Sir Hilliard's home, now that Billy thought about it, he couldn't recall meeting Mr. Bertram Marsh for himself. But there were so many Marshes; it was hard to keep track of them all.

"I hadn't seen him in years, not since I went off to university. We were never very friendly, even as children," said Freddie. "His father didn't encourage it. Uncle Kellynch—the one my cousin Kell is named after—was always at his brother Lord Marshbourne's right hand, you see, and since Kell has no brother of his own, Uncle Kellynch seemed to think that his son Bertie ought to stand beside Kell in the same way. He never liked that Kell and I were best friends and Bertie was pushed off to the side. After my parents died, Aunt Emily and Uncle Win became like another mother and father to me. I think Uncle Kellynch was afraid that they might adopt me. He saw me as a usurper, as if I'd taken the place that his son ought to have. Bertie must've had some of the same feelings, even if he wasn't very fond of Kell and Kell didn't like him."

The train had been moving more slowly during the last few minutes and now it stopped at the Downham Market station. The two young men got out onto the platform and while Freddie surrendered both their tickets to the station master, Billy retrieved their bags from the porter. They went out through the wooden gate at the end of the platform.

A smart little bright red roadster sat idling in the paved area usually reserved for cabs and luggage carts. A handsome young man with honey-colored hair and a dimpled chin was at the wheel; at the sight of the pair, he waved a hand and called out, "Freddie, old thing!"

Freddie's cousin Kell had come to meet them.

The Honourable Captain Kellynch Meredith St. George Marsh, DSO, DFC, MC, was the only son and heir to Lord Marshbourne. Since becoming an officer in the Air Corps during the final months of the war, he had grown a neat little tawny mustache that only made him look more dashing. Billy disliked him heartily. Kell Marsh was just the type to have every good thing in life come his way and receive it all as simply a matter of course. Not only had he enjoyed a brilliant and distinguished war record, but had come through it all without a scratch. So had Billy, but he resented Kell's luck on Freddie's behalf.

"Kell, hullo!" Freddie exclaimed in surprise. "How did you know which train we'd be on?"

"There aren't that many running up this sleepy little line. Besides, Mother told me about your wire. You said you'd be here in time for dinner. Come on, hop in!"

"Can all three of us fit into this contraption?" Freddie looked doubtful.

"Of course." Kell stretched one hand over his shoulder to flip open a tiny compartment on the back of the vehicle and reveal a third cushioned seat. "Your chum Billy can go in there with your bags tucked down at his feet. Plenty of room! In you go, Bill."

Billy grumbled to himself as he climbed up into the seat, but it was either squeeze himself in with the baggage or let Freddie drive off with Kell and walk the seven lonely miles between Downham Market and Marsh Hall. He had barely settled in before the little roadster zipped off. The rail station was at the edge of the town and they were soon speeding along the northward road through the flat countryside toward Marsh Hall.

"By the way, I won't be joining you for dinner," Kell announced, shouting over the putter of the car's engine. "Phil Tollarhithe's taken a room at the George and Dragon at Marshbanks, and I'm staying with him."

"I thought you and Phil had one of the cottages on the Hall grounds?" Freddie shouted back. Phillip Tollarhithe was a cousin of Kell's on his mother's side, as well as his closest friend. Phil was at Cambridge, but the last Freddie had heard he'd come to visit the Marshes during the Easter holiday break.

"We were, 'til Father threatened to toss Phil off the property. Naturally, we couldn't stay on after that."

"What happened?"

"We had a devil of row, Father and I, and I couldn't stick it another minute. He rather suspects..."

"Suspects?"

"Well, you know. About me and Phil."

Freddie did know all about Kell and Phil. "Do you want us to stay at the Inn while we're here?" he asked.

"No, you'd better go on to the Hall. Mother's expecting you. She'll be delighted to see you, and you can work on Father on my behalf. He likes you. He's always said you were a lad of uncommon sense, and he might listen to you. I'm going to need a friend, Freddie."

"Of course," responded Freddie. "But whatever for? Not over Phil?"

"No, not over Phil. There's something else I haven't told you about yet, old chap. Bertie wasn't drowned. When they pulled his body out of the river, they found he'd taken a nasty cosh to the head. The police think he was murdered. They think I did it."

***

2

After Kell had delivered this casual announcement, Freddie could only regard his cousin in amazement. "Murdered? I don't understand, Kell. Why do they think you've got something to do with Bertie's death? What proof do they have?"

"No proof," Kell answered, "but there's enough against me that looks suspicious. There was an inquest this morning. 'Murder by person or persons unknown,' they said, but I saw the way they looked at me when they said it."

"Why? Were you anywhere near the place where he drowned?"

"They think he went in just a half-mile or so from Thicket Cottage, where Phil and I were staying. You remember the end of the lane where it meets the footpath along the river? That marshy bit where the rushes grow tall and the bottom's muddy?"

A strange look came over Freddie's face. "Yes," he said, "I know it."

"Phil and I found the boat pulled up there."

"Pulled up, not washed up?"

"No. Someone had dragged it half onto the bank. There's a muddy flat below the path that's a sort of natural landing. We didn't know who'd left it there. We didn't know about Bertie's being missing. No one did, not 'til he didn't come home for dinner that night. He left the Hall from the boathouse after breakfast, and that was the last anyone saw of him. Phil and I never saw Bertie, dead or alive, but the police have it that I met him by the river. They seem to believe that I fought with him and, by accident or deliberately, hit him over the head and let him fall into the river."

"But *why*? Why do they think you fought with him?" As far as Freddie knew, even if Kell and Bertie were not on the friendliest terms, they weren't openly hostile toward each other.

"Bertie's death is only the end of it," said Kell. "I suppose all this business began when I went off to war. No, it goes even farther back than that. Father always thought highly of Bertie. Remember how he used to hold him up as an example of a properly behaved young gentleman and wonder why I couldn't be more like him? And you know what an awful old toady Bertie was! He never got into trouble. At least he never got caught out the way you and I did, and so Father never had any idea what he was really like.

"When the war began and everybody else was racing to join up and have a crack at the Huns before it was too late, Uncle Kellynch got some doctor-friend of his up in London to say that Bertie wasn't fit for fighting—a dickey heart or something of the sort. If you ask me, Bertie was worse than a Conshy. At least those conscientious objecting chaps have some principles about not wanting to kill other people and will face prison for it. Bertie just didn't want to get shot at." Kell's contempt for his cousin's cowardice was undisguised. "So while the rest of us were off risking our lives for the sake of Good Old Blighty, Bertie sat here, nice and comfy, playing at helping Father and Uncle Kell manage the estate and no doubt waiting for me to get shot down in flames. If I'd been killed in the war, like Phil's brother at the Somme, Father would naturally look to Bertie as the next in line after Uncle Kell. Uncle Kell's ambitious enough to like the idea of his son being Viscount Marshbourne one day."

"But you came home uninjured," said Freddie.

Kell grinned. "To Uncle Kell's and Bertie's great disappointment."

"If you don't mind me saying, Cap'n Kell, that sounds more like a reason for Mr. Bertram to push you into the river than the other way 'round," Billy observed from the back seat.

Kell took his eyes momentarily from the road to glance over his shoulder and that grin flashed a second time. "Maybe it was, Billy old bean. We never got on very well—Freddie can tell you about that if he hasn't already—but if Bertie bore me any grudge for surviving the war, he was smart enough to keep his feelings to himself. He said he was glad to see me alive and well, and welcomed me home just like the rest of the family. In any case, there wasn't any trouble, not 'til the day before Bertie went missing. That was when I had my quarrel with Father, the one I told you about. He threatened to disown me. He'd found out what Phil and I got up to at the cottage, you see."

"But surely he knew about that ages ago," said Freddie.

"Suspected, old thing, but he never minded it much when Phil and I were just schoolboys playing around together. Every boy who's been to public school can tell a tale or two. But Father's decided it's time for me to settle down. Since I've come home, I've had half a dozen girls paraded before me. I couldn't stand it any more. After Phil showed up at the beginning of this Easter vac, we finally had it out. I went to Father and told him that I might get married one day, but not yet. After all I've been through, I want a bit of fun. I'm not in any rush to let Phil go.

"Well, Father didn't see it that way at all. He said it was unnatural, not to mention illegal, and if I knew what was good for me I'd send Phil packing before it became a scandal. I told him I wouldn't. He said it'd be my own fault if we were arrested and he was of half a mind to summon the police himself. I dared him to. Think of what the newspapers would say: 'Viscount's Son Imprisoned on Morals Charge.' They'd never be able to prove anything, but Father's more afraid of scandal than I am. I'd never seen him so angry before. You should've heard the names he called me, and the worse names he had for poor Phil. He said he wanted Phil off his property or else he'd disown me. I left the Hall right away, and Phil and I started packing. We moved ourselves to the inn the next evening.

"Everybody knows about the quarrel—half the household must've heard Father shouting that he'd cut me off—but no one thought that much of it before Bertie's body was taken out of the river and the police started to wonder who'd wish him harm. Once they heard of my fight with Father, they came up with the idea that Father was going set me aside and put Bertie into my place, and so I must have knocked Bertie over the head and tossed him into the Marshbourne to get rid of him once and for all. Yesterday, they came round to the inn to ask me to account for my whereabouts at the time of the murder."

"Who told them about it?" asked Freddie.

"Anyone might've. It could even be Father himself, although he didn't tell them about my friendship with Phil. The detective fellow who questioned us would've been much nastier if he had. According to Mother, Father said that he wouldn't stand in the way of justice even if his own son was involved, but that's not the reason he's being so impartial. He wants to punish me, and not for anything to do with Bertie. He'd rather I be suspected of murder than be known as a pansy. At least Father can't hold Bertie over me anymore."

"Couldn't you account for where you was, Cap'n Kell?" Billy asked.

Kell shook his head. "The morning that Bertie drowned, I was off by myself. I was still upset after my row with Father. I couldn't sleep, so I got up early and went for a walk. I wanted to think things through, to figure out what to do if Father made good on his threats and Phil and I had to leave not only the cottage, but the country. I was out 'til lunchtime, nowhere near the river, but I've no proof of that. There's only my word for it." He smiled. "Phil was ready to say he'd been with me, but I wouldn't let him do it. They'd only think he was lying for my sake, which he would've been. No one's accused him of helping me to get Bertie out of the way, and I won't give them the chance to."

"How much danger are you in, Kell?" Freddie asked him seriously. "Are they really about to arrest you, or have they only been poking around?"

"Only poking around so far," Kell admitted. "I know I didn't do it, so they've no hope of finding proof that I did. I don't think they'd be so keen on me if it weren't for Father's attitude. That's the beastly part of it. The police can see that there's something more neither of us will tell them about, and of course they suspect the worst. Unless they find somebody else to suspect, they won't rest 'til they dig the truth out, and that worries me for Phil's sake as much as my own. I wouldn't begrudge the police the fun of having a murder to investigate as long as I don't go to prison at the end of it." Kell's smile faded and the brave facade dropped. Freddie and Billy saw how upset he truly was.

3

The road had followed the main course of the River Marshbourne for several miles, but then turned inland. As they neared the high stone wall that bounded the Marsh Hall park, Kell left the main road, choosing a narrow lane between tall hedgerows, and entered his family's property via a back gate. After winding through decorative woodlands and gardens, he stopped behind the stables to let Freddie and Billy off.

"I hope you won't mind if I don't take you right up to the front door, old thing," Kell said to his cousin before he drove away. "I'd rather not be seen. Give Mother my love." The roadster darted away, disappearing into the fading light under the trees.

Freddie sighed and picked up his suitcase. Billy followed with his. He'd been hearing about Marsh Hall all his life, but he'd never been here before. They went around to the other side of the stables, through a door in a hedge, and found themselves on the edge of the lawn on the Hall's garden front—an open sweep of green that stretched down to the willows that grew beside the river. Marsh Hall sat on a terrace above them.

Although the Marsh family could trace its roots back to the days of William the Conqueror, when Sieur Jocelyn de Marisco had first been granted a large portion of East Anglia in the fenlands between Ely and King's Lynn, they hadn't been prominent among the nobility in recent centuries. While the Marshes had managed to hold onto their titles and a great deal of their property, and most of them had literally kept their heads, the taint of Jacobite sympathies had prevented them from receiving higher honors. In the early 1700s, several members of the family had fled to the New World; their descendants lived in Virginia still. A younger son of the family had also been messily executed in 1586 along with Sir Anthony Babington for his part in the plot to free Mary Queen of Scots and place her on Elizabeth's throne. The Marshes and the Babington family had retained a tenuous connection since those long-ago days; Uncle Hilliard had once tried to explain to Freddie exactly how they were related to Sir Anthony, but Freddie hadn't been able to follow this tortuous branch of the family tree. The Babingtons' connection to the Marshes had grown closer when Hilliard's younger brother had married the Honourable Pamela Marsh, the youngest daughter of the last Viscount Marshbourne.

While the foundations of Marsh Hall had Tudor origins, the old manor house had been expanded into an imposing residence in the Palladian style in the 18th century. Only minor modifications, such as plumbing, electricity, and the new kitchen wing, had been added since.

Billy gaped up at the façade of the great house as the last lights of the sunset glittered in the scores of westward-facing windows.

"The old pile hasn't changed a bit," Freddie said wistfully as they approached the nearest door, at the end of the building above a curving gravel drive. "I was born at Marsh Hall, you know, and spent all my childhood here. Do you remember when Kell and I came to visit Uncle Hilliard that first time, the summer after my parents died?"

"I remember," Billy answered. As if he could forget. Billy had only been a small boy then. Sir Hilliard had not only taught him to read and write, but the peculiar old gentleman had also amused himself by giving his manservant's son poems to recite and telling him wonderful stories about fabulous, faraway places, filling his head with all sorts of nonsense that his father said would give him ideas above his place and never do him a lick of good.

When Billy had gone up to Sir Hilliard's study for his lessons on that memorable afternoon, Sir Hilliard had announced that there would be none. Instead, he had a special task for Billy. "Some young lads related to me are coming to stay for a week or two. They're boys near your own age. One of them, my nephew, in fact, has lost his mother, just as you have, Billy-boy, and his father too. I'd like you to make them welcome. Show them about. Play with them."

Billy had bashfully consented. Until that day, his only playfellows had been his elder brothers and the local farm-boys. Little gentlemen, such as the two that had arrived that same afternoon, dressed in their best clothes for their visit, high-spirited and skittish as a pair of unbroken colts, were even more strange and foreign to his experience than girls. What could he do to make friends with them?

As much as he would like to claim that he'd known from that day how important Frederick Babington would be to his future life, the truth was that at that first meeting, Billy could only tell Freddie apart from Kell in that one boy was dark-haired and the other fair. He'd learned to distinguish between them later on, when Freddie took an interest in what Sir Hilliard was teaching him and wanted to hear some of the poems he'd learned. They'd begun to be friends because of that. Kell, on the other hand, was always looking for ways to get them all into trouble.

Freddie yanked on the bell-pull beside the door. After some clanging within and an interval of silence, the imposing figure of Brambley, the Marshes' butler, appeared.

"Brambley, hello," Freddie said. "It's been quite awhile, hasn't it? I believe you're expecting me. Will you tell Aunt Emily and Uncle Win that I'm here, please?"

Brambley said, "Of course, Mr. Frederick," as he admitted the pair to the Hall, but left them standing in the vestibule with their luggage while he went "to inform My Lady of your arrival."

A few minutes later, Emily Marsh, the Viscountess Marshbourne and Kell's mother, came to greet Freddie rather than wait for him to be shown into her drawing room.

Lady Marshbourne was an attractive woman

in her middle 40s. Under normal circumstances, her strawberry-blonde curls and a certain impish spirit which her son had inherited made her seem more like a young girl than a great lady, but today her spirits were subdued. The usual sparkle in her eyes was missing, but she smiled with genuine happiness as she came forward to embrace Freddie and give him a kiss on the cheek.

"Darling boy! I've been waiting all afternoon. How good of you to come to us at this terrible time."

Freddie returned her kiss. "It's good to see you too, Aunt Emily. I'm so very sorry about Bertie."

Emily accepted his sympathies graciously. "How have you been, dear? You look so much better than you were the last time I saw you, when you were just out of hospital. You had a crutch then."

"I no longer need it, Auntie."

"I'm so glad. Poor Marcus still has his cane. They say he may always have a limp. It disturbs me when I think of what all you poor boys must've suffered, though I suppose we ought to consider ourselves lucky it hasn't been worse. Most of you have come back alive. Only poor Peter, and now Bertie, who never went to war at all." Tears shimmered in her eyes as she regarded her surviving nephew; when she averted her gaze, she noticed Billy, who had remained shyly by the door with the two suitcases. "Why, the taxicab didn't take your servant and baggage around to the service entrance?"

"We didn't come by cab, Aunt Emily," Freddie explained. "Kell brought us, but he wouldn't come in."

"No, and I don't suppose he can be blamed for feeling unwelcome in his own home. If only Win..." The corner of her mouth turned down, but she stopped herself before she said anything against her husband. "Kell must have told you the worst of this," she said confidentially to Freddie.

"Yes, Aunt Emily, and I refuse to believe a word of it. I promised Kell I'd do whatever I could to help."

"Dearest Freddie!" She gave him another kiss. "I'm certain he can count on you. You've always been his friend. I'll show you to your room, and Brambley will find a bed for your servant in the staff quarters."

"If you don't mind, Aunt Emily, I'd like Billy near me," said Freddie. "I have still my bad spells now and again, and shouldn't be left alone at night."

"You poor thing," Emily murmured sympathetically, and gave Billy serious consideration; he squirmed and colored slightly under her gaze. At last, she said, "Yes, I think that can be arranged. Brambley, the big guest room near the master suite instead of the blue room. That will do."

Brambley said, "Yes, My Lady," and picked up Freddie's bag. Billy carried his own.

"I had put Charles Burke in that room, but he won't mind moving to the smaller one for you," Emily said as she led this small procession up the stairs. "There's a cot in the dressing room your servant can use."

"Thank you, Auntie. I didn't know Chubbs was here. And Louisa?"

Charles and Louisa Burke were no blood

relation of Freddie's, but their father's sister had married his Uncle Kellynch and had been Bertie's mother. They had been frequent visitors at Marsh Hall as children and Freddie thought of them as his cousins as much as any of the young Marshes. Charles had been a rather rotund boy in the days when he and Freddie were at school together, provoking the nickname of "Chubbs," which remained long after he'd outgrown his childhood chubbiness.

"He came down from Oxford the day before yesterday. Louisa's been visiting since Easter with their Aunt Beatrice. They'll all be delighted to see you." They had gone up two flights and half-way down a long corridor. Emily stopped outside a closed door and Brambley stepped forward to open it and carry Freddie's luggage inside. "The bath is just across the hallway," she informed Freddie, "but I'll have some hot water sent up to you so that you can wash quickly before dinner." She squeezed his hand. "I'll leave you to freshen up."

After she and Brambley had gone, Freddie had a quick look around the large and comfortable room, with its view of the gardens and a few of Chubbs' possessions left lying about, then peeked through the connecting door into the dressing room. "Will you be comfortable with that little bed, Billy?" he asked.

Billy joined him at the dressing-room doorway: the spare bed tucked between the massive chest of drawers and towering wardrobe was small, but no smaller than the one he'd slept in for years in the room he'd shared with his brothers. "I had worse," he said.

Freddie chuckled. "That awful little dugout

off the trenches? You remember how often we slept beneath the cots for fear of getting hit by a shell in our sleep. Anything after that is pure luxury."

"We got spoiled since we came home," said Billy, joining in the joke. He was relieved that Freddie was able to laugh about those horrible days.

There was a knock on the door. Billy let in the maidservant, who had brought up the promised can of hot water. "You'd better hurry up and wash and I'll lay out your things," he said as he poured some water into the china washbasin on its stand. "You won't want to be late for dinner."

4

"Freddie, hello!" Chubbs Burke cried out in surprise and delight as Freddie came down the main stairway to the landing outside the dining room. No longer a chubby boy, he had grown into a hearty, broad-shouldered young man, several inches taller than his friend. Chubbs looked more like a soldier than a serious scholar even though he'd discarded his uniform more than two years ago when he resumed his studies. The scar left by a bullet's grazing his left cheek was the only visible sign remaining of his war experience. "I say, old man! I didn't know you'd joined us."

"Only just arrived," said Freddie, "but I'd heard that you were here."

"Just a day or two myself, but Aunt Beatrice and Louisa–" Chubbs nodded his head to indicate his sister, "have been at the Hall for awhile. Uncle Winthrop invited them specially, before all this trouble began." He lowered his voice at these last words.

Louisa Burke, a mousy-haired and petite girl, came forward shyly to welcome Freddie. She'd been a schoolgirl in pigtails the last time he'd seen her, but she was now a young lady of twenty. Freddie then received a kiss from Aunt Beatrice and murmured his condolences about the tragic loss of her nephew Bertie. They went together into the dining room, where the rest of the family was assembling for dinner.

The Viscount Winthrop St. John Marsh, Lord Marshbourne, stood beside his chair at the head of the table, waiting for the others to take their places. He was a heavy-set, florid-faced, fair-haired man, and a good prediction of what his son Kell might become in 25 or 30 years, given a sedentary life and several large meals every day. Kellynch Marsh, Winthrop's younger brother and Bertie's father, was like Winthrop in looks, but shorter with sandy hair that was noticeably thinning on top.

Stephen Marsh, the third brother, was taller and thinner and wore a pair of spectacles over his kindly but unfocused blue eyes. As the youngest son, he'd been educated as a clergyman and was intended for the family living at St. Botolph's-on-the-Marshland upon his ordination. While a student at Cambridge, however, he'd fallen under the influence of Sir Hilliard and taken more interest in classical literature and mythology than in modern theology. Once he had passed his exams, he'd returned home to marry Matilda Grant, the daughter of the vicar holding his promised living, and showed no signs of wishing his father-in-law to retire or of taking up residence at the vicarage.

His chief interest for the past twenty years had laid in seeking the common origins of myths and legends from various ancient cultures with an eye toward eventual publication of his work. He had named his sons Daedalus and Icarus; his daughter Cecilia had narrowly escaped being christened Alcippe, but Matilda had put her foot down. Once they were old enough to go to school, Daedalus and Icarus had been renamed Dotty and Bicky by the other boys and were thereafter called so by everyone, even their father.

The boys, seated on either side of their mother, had been born two years apart; Dotty was twenty-one now and Bicky nineteen, but they looked enough alike to be twins with their square-jawed faces and dark brown hair grown long enough in front to fall over their eyes. Too young to participate in the war, they retained a youthful innocence and liveliness of spirit that their older cousins had lost. Like Phil Tollarhithe, they were students at Cambridge but home for the holiday.

Aunt Theresa arrived late with her younger daughter Amelia. Theresa was a strikingly tall and poised woman in her 50s with streaks of grey in her carefully coiled hair. Amelia was a pretty girl of twenty-two, lacking her mother's height but thoroughly modern with her bobbed brunette hair and a skirt that showed her knees. She looked wan today and rather strained; there were circles under her expressive brown eyes. Her father, Martin Marsh, was from the American branch of the family and had come to Europe in the 1880s on the Grand Tour. While visiting his English relatives, he'd fallen in love with his ancestral home—not to mention Miss Theresa Portleigh from one of the neighboring county families—and stayed on until his death ten years ago. His wife and three grown children, Marcus, Agatha, and Amelia, still made Marsh Hall their home.

"I'm afraid Agatha isn't feeling well," Theresa apologized for the absence of her elder daughter as she took her accustomed chair. "She doesn't want dinner and prefers to stay in her room tonight."

There were some murmurs of sympathy, but the incident which must be foremost on all their minds wasn't discussed over dinner. Whether it was grief over Bertie, worry for Kell, or their awareness of the footmen in attendance at the table, the Marshes kept their emotions reserved. The depth of distress felt during this family tragedy was indicated primarily by how little appetite anyone had. The ladies picked over course after course, but even Winthrop was seen to push away his main course half finished. Once everyone had expressed their welcome to Freddie and asked after his health, the conversation turned to the recent marriage of Stephen and Matilda's daughter Cecilia and Theresa's son Marcus, neither of whom was present that night.

"I was sorry to have missed the wedding," said Freddie. It had occurred last autumn, at the beginning of his relapse. He'd been astounded at the news of his cousins' marriage, though he wouldn't dream of saying so.

"We all missed you, my dear," said Matilda. "It's a pity you weren't here. Father performed the ceremony at his church. It was quite beautiful, and the grandest ball we've had in years afterwards. Almost like the old days."

"It's a very good match," said Winthrop. "Celia and Marcus are the first children of the Hall to marry, but it's just the sort of thing we hope to see from all you young people."

"Do you have any plans for marriage yourself, Freddie?" Beatrice asked him. "Is there some nice girl you've got an eye on?"

"No– No one in particular," Freddie answered, blushing more than the innocent question warranted. "Where is the– ah– young couple now? I thought that they were living here."

"They're at one of the cottages up the river," said Theresa. "Marcus took it before he married— to have a little peace and quiet, he said. He's writing about his experiences in the war, you know."

"A lot of men are," said Freddie. Uncle Hilliard had suggested that he do so himself as a way of formalizing his worst memories and perhaps laying them to rest in his mind.

"He and Celia settled there after they returned from their honeymoon, and have stayed on these past six months."

"You'll see them tomorrow," added Stephen. "They'll be returning to the house for the funeral."

There was an awkward silence.

Now that the taboo had been breached, the subject could be discussed. Amelia was the first to speak. "What will happen to Kell if the police arrest him?" she asked tentatively.

Emily made a small sound of distress.

"You needn't be frightened for the boy, my dear," her husband hastened to reassure her. "I don't believe it will come to that."

"The police must be mistaken," said Theresa. "There can be nothing in these terrible suspicions against Kell. I'm positive that some outsider must have done it. Some tramp wandering the woods."

"It can't be true," Louisa agreed softly. "Not Kell."

"I don't believe it was murder at all," said Chubbs. "The police will find that this was an accident, I'm sure of it. Boats can be dangerous things, especially these little skiffs." Chubbs was an expert punter and captain of his college rowing team. "I don't know how many poor beggars who take a spill into the Cherwell we pull out every summer, and that's quite a tame little stream when compared to the Marshbourne."

"Bertie knew his way around a skiff as well as you do, Charles," said Uncle Kellynch.

"I don't deny it, Uncle. Every one of us learned how to handle an oar as soon as we were old enough to play about in the boathouse. But the Marshbourne is a difficult river. To go out rowing alone and tell no one where you're going, the way Bertie did, is asking for trouble."

"As I see it, the difficulty is that Kell can't prove he was somewhere else when poor Bertie was drowned," said Dotty. "That's why the police suspect him, isn't it, Uncle Winthrop? But what's in that? Who can ever account for their time, as if we knew in advance that something horrible was going to happen and we must always be prepared to defend ourselves against accusations? Can anyone here say where they were that morning?" He looked at the others around the table. "If the police had troubled to ask me, I couldn't have given them a better answer than Kell's. No, my story is even more suspicious, for I was out upon the river too. I went fishing that morning down at the Upper Lock pool." His gaze landed on his younger brother and, with a note of teasing, he asked, "And where were you, Bicky?"

"You know I was up in our bedroom," his brother answered with a little huff. "I slept in rather late. Can I prove it? I don't suppose so, not unless someone heard me snoring. Did anyone, Dotty?"

"I'm sure I couldn't say," Dotty replied, "but you do snore rather loudly. Someone must have heard. Now, what about the rest of you?"

"I went out for a walk," said Amelia.

Louisa opened her mouth as if she wanted to say something, but a glance from Aunt Beatrice stopped her; she blushed and began to rearrange the vegetables on her plate with her fork.

"I wasn't here at all," Chubbs contributed. "I was at home in my digs at Oxford."

"Not good enough, Chubbs!" said Dotty. "You might easily have driven over."

"I don't like this game of yours," Kellynch said darkly. "I don't find it at all funny."

"You are being rather thoughtless, Daedalus," reproved Stephen; the rare use of his son's full name showed that he was serious. "This isn't a detective story."

Dotty immediately looked contrite. "I am sorry, Father, Uncle Kell. It wasn't meant to be a game. I only wanted to show that any one of us might be suspected as easily as Kell, and for reasons just as flimsy. If the police have nothing more than that against Kell, then they'd be better off looking for somebody else who might've wanted to harm Bertie."

***

5

After dinner the ladies retired, either to their beds or the drawing room. Stephen returned to his researches in the library. The young men planned to walk over to Marshbanks for a drink at the pub; Freddie meant to accompany them, when Winthrop turned to him and said, "Frederick, it's been quite some time since we've had a talk. Why don't you join us in the study?"

In the days of the last Lord Marshbourne, Freddie's grandfather Roderick, it had been an established evening custom for the gentlemen of the house to settle down to smoke and enjoy a glass of port after dinner; Winthrop had carried on this tradition. While Freddie would've preferred to go out with his cousins and perhaps see Kell and Phillip at the inn before the evening grew too late, he realized that if he was going to be of any help to Kell, he needed to be in his uncle's company. "Yes, thank you, Uncle Win. I will."

The children had always been forbidden to play in the master's study, and Freddie felt a little strange as he followed Kellynch and Winthrop inside. In spite of his experiences in the Great War, this invitation from his uncle made him feel as if he were truly considered one of the adults. He'd only been called into this room full of musty books and ledgers before on serious matters: Here, he and Kell had been scolded and received punishments for whatever mischief they'd gotten themselves into, and he had occasionally discussed business concerning the property his parents had left him. As Freddie's legal guardian, Winthrop had managed things for him before he'd come of age. It had been a point of pride for Winthrop to give scrupulous attention to the finances of the orphan in his care. No one could accuse him of mishandling the boy's affairs. Freddie recalled that his uncle had been especially proud to say that he could hand everything over to Freddie when he came of age in a better condition than it'd been in when he'd taken charge of it. That was the last time Freddie had been in this room, on his 18th birthday, just before he'd gone to university.

He sank into one of the overstuffed leather chairs near the fire. He'd left his cigarette case upstairs in the pocket of the coat he'd been wearing on the train, but Winthrop offered him a pipe from the rack on the mantelpiece, and then poured out three glasses of port from a decanter on the sideboard.

As he handed Freddie one of the glasses, Winthrop patted his shoulder. "It's times like this I'm glad you're back among us, my boy. You've been sorely missed—not only by your Aunt Emily and your cousins, but by us as well." Winthrop sounded warm and sincere, but his brother didn't appear as pleased at Freddie's return. "I don't suppose you've given much thought to what you're going to do with yourself?"

"No, Uncle Win," Freddie answered. "I sometimes think I'd like to go back to the university and complete my degree once I'm quite well enough, but it would feel very odd to carry on with it at my age among the twenty-year-old boys." He felt that way around Dotty and Bicky as well as Phil Tollarhithe; though only a few years younger than he, they seemed like children. Too young for the war, they were as much a part of a different generation as his uncles were. "Uncle Hill is very keen on it."

"I daresay he's right," Winthrop said grudgingly. He thought Sir Hilliard peculiar and didn't entirely approve of his intellectual pursuits. "You ought to have some sort of occupation. I know you've been through some bad times, but that's the best way for you to put them behind you—look to your future! The war was a disruptive experience for all of you young men, but you've got to carry on. That's the only thing to do. You're not children anymore. It's time you settled down into your lives. Kell has to realize that. He can't go on playing the naughty schoolboy forever. Your Aunt Emily's told me that you've seen him today."

"Yes, sir. He met me at the train. I intend to stand by him until he's been cleared of this awful suspicion. You don't think he's guilty, do you?" Freddie looked from one uncle to the other.

"I wouldn't like to say so in front of Emily and the other ladies," said Uncle Kellynch, "and I don't say Kell is responsible for my boy's death, but if he is, then hanging's too good for him."

"Oh, I'm sure it won't come to *that*. There are a few things that look bad against Kell, but it'll all be cleared up soon enough," Winthrop answered confidently. "Of course, I can't stand in the way of the police investigation. There must be no question of special favors. That's only fair. Justice must be seen to be done. The Marshbourne heir shouldn't be treated differently from any common murder suspect. It'll be a lesson for the boy. Kell's always been too flighty."

"He gets it from his mother," said Kellynch. "I told you there'd be trouble one day when you married a Tollarhithe, Win."

"Emily was a flighty girl in her youth," Winthrop admitted, "but she's grown much steadier as she's matured and I've never had any reason to complain of her conduct. You can't hold her responsible for our son's wild behavior."

"You've both been too indulgent with him. The boy should've been reined in," Kellynch responded. "It may be too late for him now. It's certainly too late for my Bertie."

"Kell still has a chance, if we give him one," Winthrop said, and turned to refill Freddie's glass. "You're a sensible young man, Freddie. You know what responsibility is. Can't you talk to Kell? Make him see reason."

Freddie had to smile. "Kell asked me to talk to you, Uncle. He told me about your- ah- quarrel."

"That's just the sort of thing I mean!" With a glance at his brother, Winthrop leaned closer to Freddie and spoke barely above a whisper. "I don't mind Phillip Tollarhithe. He's not a bad lad, but he's not the most suitable companion I could choose for my son. He's young and impressionable, and too easily led by a stronger personality. He lets Kell get away with too much, and there are limits to what decency will stand. The stories I've heard about what goes on at that cottage! Whether or not a word of it's true, it's gone too far this time, Freddie, and it's got to stop before it leads to serious trouble. Kell must realize that. There's only so much I can do to protect him."

"If Kell does agree to break with Phil-" Freddie asked, although he was quite certain that Kell would never accept his father's terms, "will you protect him, Uncle? Tell the police to leave him alone unless they can produce some proof against him?"

"Oh, I couldn't do that," said Winthrop. "It wouldn't be right for me to impede them in the course of their duties, even for the sake of my son. But if they can't produce anything against him soon, I might suggest that they consider turning their attention elsewhere. That's only fair."

6

When Freddie returned to his room, he found Chubbs' possessions had been removed. Billy was crouched before the chest of drawers in the dressing room, putting away the clothes from Freddie's suitcase. A suit of blue pajamas and a quilted dressing gown had been laid out across the foot of Freddie's bed. Freddie could see that the doors to the wardrobe were open and Billy had hung up one of his best shirts, freshly pressed, along with his black frock-coat and a pale gray waistcoat to be worn for his cousin's funeral.

"I'd almost forgotten that we came here for a funeral," he said as he flopped down across the bed. "Poor Bertie. I've hardly given him a thought at all. I can't think of anything except how to help Kell since we heard he was in trouble." He lay his head in the crook of one arm; he felt very weary, and the glasses of port he'd had with his uncles had gone straight to his head. "I'd hoped to go and see Kell and Phillip tonight, but I'm too tired now for the walk to Marshbanks."

"That's no surprise, not after the day you had," said Billy, and shut the drawers of the chest.

"You scarce had a minute to catch your breath since we got here." He came into Freddie's room and shoved aside the clothing laid out there to sit on the foot of the bed. "You're not up to worrying yourself. You know you're not. It takes too much out of you. When you start fretting, it gets to buzzing around inside your head, then you have one of your bad spells and wake up screaming from those nightmares you have."

Freddie sighed. "I know. I'll try to rest tomorrow before the funeral. But I must do what I can for Kell. It's too important to be set aside, Billy, no matter how it affects me."

"Is Cap'n Kell in that much trouble?" asked Billy. "Did you talk to his Lordship about him, like you said you would?"

"I've just spent the most awful hour in conference with Uncle Win." Freddie sat up. "Oh, Billy, you should have heard him. Kell understands his father all too well. Uncle Win doesn't believe for a minute that Kell's guilty of this crime. He's punishing him for their quarrel over Phillip. He practically told me that he could have the police set aside their case against Kell at a word, but he won't do it. He wants to teach 'the boy' a lesson by letting them question and harass him. I can't talk him out of it—in fact, Uncle Win wants me to talk to Kell and convince him to give Phillip up. Then there's Uncle Kellynch, who's doing his best to poison his brother's mind against Kell. I heard him do it. He never misses a chance to remind Uncle Win how wild and irresponsible Kell is. I can see now where Bertie learned that sort of thing."

"An 'awful old toady' Cap'n Kell called his cousin," Billy remembered the conversation in the roadster.

"That's just what Bertie was as a boy. A toady. He made up to the grown-ups. One doesn't like to speak ill of the dead..." Freddie hesitated, and then did so. If he couldn't tell Billy the truth, who could he confide in? "Bertie used to tattle on us. He was always running off to his father or mine or Uncle Win to tell them what mischief Kell and I were up to and made it sound worse than it really was. We used to find ways to sneak around him, so that he couldn't prove his tattling-tales. I thought we'd outgrown such childish tricks years ago." He lifted his head and looked up at Billy. "But, do you know, it wouldn't surprise me to learn that Bertie had carried tales about Kell and Phil to Kell's father—and put their friendship in the ugliest possible light, if Uncle Win's reaction is any indication. Goodness knows what sort of Sodom and Gomorrah he believes those two have been getting up to at Thicket Cottage."

"Cap'n Kell," Billy ventured carefully onto this delicate subject. "He talks pretty bold about him 'n' Mr. Phillip."

"Why shouldn't he, to me?" responded Freddie. "We're as close as brothers and we've kept each other's secrets since we were old enough to have any. I've known that he and Phil have been– well– especially close since Kell took him under his wing at Eton."

"But there was talk about Cap'n Kell before that."

"Yes, that's true. Kell was rather notorious as a boy. It's a wonder he wasn't expelled. Phil's settled him down. If they're happy together, I don't see why it should be anyone's business but their own. They shouldn't have to be afraid of being arrested for it—it's another one of those abominable and antiquated Victorian laws that ought to be chucked on the bonfire. But Kell feels free to confide in me. He trusts me implicitly... as I trust you, Billy. You wouldn't go running off to the police with tales about them, would you?"

Billy was startled and disconcerted as Freddie's eyes suddenly gazed intensely into his.

"No!" he insisted. "I'd never carry tales." He had no affection or feelings of loyalty for Kell Marsh, but he knew that Freddie would never forgive him. He'd see it as a betrayal of their friendship. And there was something more, a memory that gnawed at the back of Billy's mind. How much did Freddie recall of the day he'd been wounded?

But Freddie had turned that intense gaze away from him. "Good lad," he said. "You know how I rely on you. And Kell's depending on me. None of the family believes he had anything to do with Bertie's death, except perhaps for Uncle Kellynch, but they'll only sit and wait for the police investigation to take its course. I can't sit by with them. It's too dangerous. I'm going to look into this matter myself."

"Like one o' them detecting fellers you read about?"

Freddie laughed. "I suppose so." Where had that absurd idea come from? It must be the port. And yet... "Well, why not? How difficult can it be? I only need a good eye for observation and some common sense. It's not as if I intend to catch Bertie's murderer—that, I leave to the police. But perhaps I can find some proof of Kell's innocence, something that will turn their attention away from him before they dig too deeply into his private affairs and his quarrel with Uncle Win. You'll help me, won't you, Billy? You can be my Watson!"

"Your what?"

"Watson. Watkins. It's very close. Only you aren't a doctor. You can help me find out things. Be my eyes and ears in places where I can't go." Freddie gave the problem of how precisely Billy could assist him some minutes' thought before he asked, "You had your dinner in the servants' hall, didn't you?"

Billy nodded, although he didn't see the point of this question.

"Was there any gossip? What do the servants think of this business?"

"They talked of nothing else! They're all for Cap'n Kell. They say he's a bit wild but good-hearted and would never do such a thing. Now, the other one, Mr. Bertram..." Billy trailed off in embarrassment.

Freddie looked curious. "What about 'the other one'? I'd like to hear their opinion of Bertie too."

"Well, his Lordship might've had a high opinion of him, but according to them in the servants' hall, Mr. Bertram Marsh wasn't the proper little gentleman he made himself out to be. They say he was something of a caution with the pretty maids."

"Was he? That's a possibility I hadn't thought of." Freddie considered it. "If there was some maid that Bertie was trifling with, perhaps an outraged father or brother or jilted sweetheart tried to put a stop to it, and went too far."

"And there's more," Billy told him, then hesitated again.

"What, Billy? Out with it."

"It's second-hand news, you might say. One of the undercooks is sister to a farmer that lives on the other side of the river, and she went to visit him this morning on her day off. At dinner, she was telling how her brother said he'd seen a boy and a pretty, dark-haired girl, rowing up the river the day your cousin went missing. She has it that it must've been Mr. Bertram, up to something."

"Bertie had a girl with him?" Freddie cried. "Can that be true? Everyone in the family seems to think he went out alone."

"It mightn't be so," Billy said. "Like I was saying, it's second hand and not everybody believed it. Some of `em down in the servants' hall said that the cook's brother was making up a tale to make himself important. And then someone else said it must've been this girl, and not Cap'n Kell, who pushed Mr. Bertie into the water, and some more of `em agreed with that. They said the cook ought to tell the police about it, and the ones who didn't believe it said there wasn't nothing to tell and she'd best keep her mouth shut. They was quarreling over it when I came away."

"It could be a fuss over nothing," Freddie had to agree. "It might've been another boy and girl. Lots of courting couples go out boating on the Marshbourne." He lay down again, pillowing his head on his arm and shutting his eyes, but he was still thinking. After awhile, he said, "But, Billy, what if it's true? Who could she be?"

***

7

The next morning immediately after breakfast, Freddie set out to walk to the village of Marshbanks. Billy, as usual, accompanied him. They took the broad, gravel path that led away from the Hall northward through the gardens; after they'd gone about a quarter-mile and passed through a band of trees, Freddie opened a gate and went through. They had emerged at the corner of a meadow near the river.

The River Marshbourne, like most waterways in the Fen country, had long ago been diverted into channels to drain the primeval marshlands, cutting the countryside for miles around into a patchwork of squares, but here along Marsh Hall, it retained its natural course. The only modification made was a raised earthwork embankment to protect the property from flooding. Freddie climbed up onto this embankment. A footpath bordered by tall grass and long-stemmed blue and white asters ran atop it and, below, a grassy slope led down to the water's edge. Rushes grew close to the bank, except for one broad, flat muddy area that had been cleared to provide a boat landing.

"I thought we were going to see Cap'n Kell and Mr. Phillip," Billy said when he caught up.

"We are," answered Freddie, "but I wanted to stop here first. I wanted to see where Kell and Phil found Bertie's boat. If I'm going to look into this matter myself, it seems like the best place to start." He stood looking out over the broad expanse of the river glittering in the sun as he spoke. "This isn't very far from where my parents drowned."

Billy now understood the odd look that had

crossed Freddie's face when Kell had described this place. Freddie rarely spoke of the incident, but Billy remembered hearing about it when he was a little boy. There had been some sort of terrible and mysterious accident, leaving the Babingtons' ten-year-old son an orphan to be brought up by his Marsh relatives.

"Were you here to see when it happened?" he asked.

Freddie shook his head. "I was up at the Hall, playing with Kell and the other children in the nursery. I didn't hear about it 'til the next morning. Aunt Emily took me aside and told me she had some bad news and I must be very brave. It's a treacherous part of the river, even without foul play. Because of the mud, you can't see the bottom and it drops very suddenly from the shallows, where those rushes are, to the deeps. The surface of the water looks quite calm out there, but the currents are very strong. You can be pulled under..." He took his eyes from the river and looked down at the bank immediately below where he was standing to find a long, flat scrape in the mud. "The boat was drawn up there." He pointed. "Bertie's body was found much farther downriver, but he must've gone into the water near this spot. Why do you suppose he got out here?"

"Maybe he was visiting somebody," Billy suggested.

"Who?" Both young men turned to consider the cottages visible along a winding lane that led away through the trees. "Kell and Phil? It's possible. He might've intended to go to Thicket Cottage to see them after the quarrel—to offer his condolences or to gloat—but I don't think they were expecting him to call. Kell would've said so if they had, and they would've guessed who the boat belonged to when they found it."

"Does anybody else live out this way?"

"Two of my cousins were just married and have set up house in one of the cottages. Bertie might've meant to visit them, but I can't imagine that they had any part in this. A newlywed pair of murderers doesn't sound very likely. And there are others who keep cottages out here. Old Uncle Nicholas retired to his cottage years ago and is hardly ever seen at the Hall. My cousin Agatha used to have a studio, and still does for all I know."

"Studio?" Billy echoed.

"She paints." All around the scraped area where the boat had landed was a churn of multiple shoe prints; Freddie scrambled down the slope and crouched to examine these more closely. "I wish I could tell something by the footprints, but there are so many of them. It looks like half of the county has been trampling here."

"I bet that Sherlock Holmes you're always reading about could look at that muddle and say who those feet all belonged to," Billy said as he joined Freddie by the river.

"Yes, and how long ago each was here and what they were all up to," Freddie agreed. "Unfortunately, he isn't on this case. We'll have to puzzle it out ourselves, my dear Watkins. I can't hope to do as well, but I think I can deduce that one set of these footprints is Bertie's. Two of the others are certainly Kell's and Phil's, and that huge boot-print there must belong to the local constable. Billy, look! There's a bare set of footprints here, under the rest of the muddle."

Billy looked where his friend was pointing. The round indents of bare toes and a heel were distinctly visible. "They look pretty small."

"Yes. A woman's foot, surely." Freddie pursued the idea with growing excitement as his imagination took flight. "If he wasn't visiting one of the family cottages, perhaps Bertie came here to meet with some girl from Marshbanks or one of the neighboring farms." He rose from his crouched position and walked slowly along the river's edge with his eyes on the ground, trying to follow the traces of the bare footprints that hadn't been totally obscured by the shoes and boots that had walked over the same spot afterwards; he hadn't gone five yards from the place where the boat had landed when he spotted a metallic glint in the muddy water. "Here, what's that?"

Billy watched anxiously as Freddie stripped off his own shoes and socks to wade out into the shallows amid the rushes. The water only washed around Freddie's calves, but he had spoken mere minutes ago of how treacherous this part of the river was. "Don't go out no deeper." Billy warned him. "You know I can't swim if you fall in."

"I won't." Freddie had bent over and was reaching down into the mud; he brought up something that glittered in the sunlight and swished it around in the water to rinse it clean.

"What'd you find?" asked Billy.

Freddie waded back to the shore to show him: an ornamental fragment made up of three swirls of silver shaped like tiny leaves intertwined. Within each curl of silver was set a red garnet. "It looks like part of an earring or perhaps a lady's brooch. So a woman *was* here!" he cried triumphantly. "Do you suppose this belongs to the mysterious girl your cook's brother claims he saw in the boat with Bertie?"

"That might've fallen there at any time," Billy pointed out. "You said yourself that too many people've been on this spot since Mr. Bertram's boat was found. Anybody could've dropped it, before or afterwards."

"It can't have been in the water for very long," Freddie countered. "The silver isn't tarnished."

"But if it fell before, why didn't the police find it?"

"They may not have been looking for it," Freddie answered after giving the question some thought. "Everyone thought that Bertie's death was an accident at first, and if they lit upon Kell soon after they found the body downriver, they mayn't have come back to this spot to look for clues. It wouldn't mean anything to them. They haven't heard the story about the girl in the boat." Then he sighed. "Well, you're probably right, Billy. It may have nothing to do with the murder, but maybe..." He tucked the broken piece of jewelry into his coat pocket. "It can't hurt to keep hold of it."

8

As they climbed down from the embankment, a feminine voice called out from the small garden in front of the nearest cottage, "Freddie, hello! When did you get here?"

A pretty girl with dark brown curls cut short and held back from her face by a broad band of black ribbon came up to the garden gate and held out one hand to him over it.

"Celia," Freddie went to her. "How are you? How is married life?"

Cecilia Marsh was the "baby" of the Marsh brood, only seventeen. Freddie was astonished that she'd been the first to marry. He still thought of her as a schoolgirl. In fact, she had only just come out of school last summer; letters he'd received from her mother and aunts mentioned their hopes of a coming-out ball at the beginning of the Season— finally, a return to the way things had been before the war—but instead of making her debut, Celia had quietly been married in November. To Marcus, of all people! Marcus Marsh was thirty. Such an unexpected and hasty match naturally suggested to Freddie that Celia was going to have a baby, though Marcus seemed an unlikely seducer. If that were so, however, she showed no signs of it. She and Marcus had been married for five months; if she'd been pregnant at the time of her wedding, surely she would be showing by now. On the contrary, her figure in her trim little black dress remained girlishly slender. Had she lost her child? Had there ever been one? Freddie doubted he'd ever learn the truth of the matter.

"It's simply divine!" Celia answered his question. "You can't know how wonderful it is having a home that's all my own, even if it's only four little rooms. Like a doll's house. We're about to go back to the Hall for poor Bertie's funeral." She turned as her husband emerged from the cottage, carrying a carpet-bag, and said, "Darling, look who it is!"

"Freddie. D'you do," Marcus mumbled gruffly and nodded his head to his cousin.

Unlike his thoroughly modern young wife

and his sister Amelia, Marcus was determinedly old-fashioned. He held himself with the rigidity of a tight-laced Victorian of the strictest moral character. He'd been shot in the knee in 1916 and his recovery had been long and painful; he still used a brass-headed cane. The stiffness in his right leg increased his rigidity, as did the buttoned black coat and high collar he wore for the funeral, but Freddie had seen him as apparently inflexible in comfortable old tweeds long before he'd been wounded.

"Are you staying at the Hall?" Celia asked Freddie.

"Yes, I just arrived last night. We're on our way to Marshbanks to see Kell and Phillip."

Marcus snorted at the mention of Kell and Phillip, and took the baggage around to a shelter at the side of the cottage, where a motorbike with sidecar sat under a tarp.

"You mustn't mind him," Celia apologized for her husband's bad manners. "He never approved of Kell, and now–! Isn't it horrible?"

"Awful," Freddie agreed.

"But I don't believe Kell would ever do such a thing. I don't see how he had the chance. He was never by the river that morning, as far as I could see."

"So you didn't see Kell pass toward the river?" Freddie asked, then turned to include Marcus, who was walking the motorbike out into the lane. "Did either of you see anyone?"

"No," Marcus answered. "No one who hadn't a reason to be there."

"We did see Kell and Phillip, but that was well after noon," added Celia. "I'm certain that Kell never came this way earlier."

"Were you here all that morning?" asked Freddie.

"What d'you mean?" Marcus asked back.

"Only that if you were out, you might've missed seeing something important," Freddie replied, "something that will help Kell. I want to help him, if I can."

"We were here," said Celia. "Marcus was writing in his study, and I was in our darling little front parlor for the longest time after breakfast. Of course I didn't sit and stare out the window every minute. I never saw anyone pass by. I wish I had. I'd tell the police and Uncle Winthrop that."

As she came out through the gate, Freddie asked her, "By the way, Ceel, have you lost any jewelry? I found a broken earring by the river." He took it out of his pocket. "Could it be yours?"

The girl stared at the fragment of jewelry in the palm of Freddie's hand and shook her head. "No, that isn't mine." Freddie thought she sounded reluctant, as if she weren't telling all the truth. "I haven't been near the river in ages. Marcus doesn't like to go boating."

"But Bertie did?" Freddie asked softly.

"Oh, yes," Celia answered, and tears welled in her eyes. "Poor Bertie. I'll miss him. He was such fun—but," she insisted with sudden urgency, "that was all such a long time ago!"

"Celia, come on!" Marcus summoned her. "Are you riding with me, or will you walk?" A churlishness in his tone implied that he resented her ability to walk the short distance to Marsh Hall with ease.

"Of course I'll ride with you, darling." With another glance of apology at Freddie, Celia ran to join her husband. "We'll see you at the Hall later," she called over her shoulder as she climbed into the sidecar.

"She's got dark hair," Billy observed once the newlyweds had driven up the lane in the direction of the main road. "And I'll bet anything you like she's been out boating on the river with Mr. Bertram."

Freddie couldn't disagree; that was the impression he'd gotten as well. "I don't think Celia could kill anybody," he said. "She can be a silly little chit, but she's harmless. Besides, she sounded genuinely sorry that Bertie's dead. It doesn't seem that very many people are." But a tickle of suspicion at the back of his mind suddenly made his joke about murderous newlyweds seem not so funny anymore. The newly-married couple wouldn't commit murder together, but if Bertie had been paying attentions to Celia before her marriage—or even afterwards—who knew how her humorless husband might react? The idea was disturbing. He didn't want to suspect such a horrible thing of any of his cousins.

A little farther down the lane was a shabbier cottage with an untrimmed hedge. An elderly man was standing in the small front garden, his pipe clenched between his teeth as he concentrated intensely on practicing his golf swing.

"Uncle Nicholas, hello!" Freddie shouted out loudly enough for the old man to hear. Nicholas Marsh was his great-uncle, the younger brother of the late Roderick, Lord Marshbourne.

Nicholas looked up, squinted in Freddie's direction, then burst into a smile. "Is that young Freddie? Pammy's boy?"

"Yes, it is." Freddie went up to the hedge and pushed some of the untrimmed branches down to look over the top. "It's good to see you, Uncle Nick."

Nicholas tucked his golf club under one arm and stepped over a number of golf-balls scattered in the grass to come to the hedge and speak to his great-nephew. "It's been quite some time since I last saw you, but I'd know you anywhere, my lad. You're the image of your mother, poor Pam." He shook his head sadly at the memory of his long-dead niece. "You're here for the funeral?"

"Yes, that's right." But Freddie observed that his uncle was wearing a battered and patched old tweed jacket and flannel trousers. "Aren't you going to attend yourself?"

"Oh, I suppose I'll have to go for appearances' sake," said Nicholas, "but I'm not going to the Hall before or after. I'm missing my visit to the course today as it is. The service'll be bad enough to listen to—I couldn't stand to hear all the women sobbing and everyone going on about how wonderful young Bertram Marsh was, when it wasn't the case at all." Freddie's eyes widened at this frank admission, and his great-uncle continued. "Now, you haven't been home in awhile, lad. You didn't see how Bertie was doing his best to take what was Kell's rightful place while Kell was off to war. It was disgusting, seeing how he wormed his way into Winthrop's good graces."

"But surely he was set aside once Kell returned," said Freddie.

"He was, but I know he didn't give up trying, nor had his father. They meant for Bertie to be the next Lord Marshbourne. I don't claim that Kell knocked him into the river, but if he did, then Bertie had it coming. I'd say he got what he deserved, whoever did it." Nicholas gave a golf-ball on the grass near his feet a good whack and sent it across the lawn into an overgrown herbaceous border. "I hear that Kell's left for the village." Freddie confirmed that this was true. "If you see him, mind you tell him I said so. I'm on his side in this."

"Yes, Uncle. I will."

"And the way he chased after girls," the old gentleman went on speaking of Bertie. "None of the local girls were safe with him. A disgrace. Why, I saw one myself just the other day, running up this very lane from the river. If Bertie was chasing her, I can guess what that upstart was after her for!"

"A girl?" asked Freddie, suddenly alert. "What girl?"

"I couldn't say. She went by very quickly, and my eyes aren't what they used to be. I don't know who she was."

"Was she dark-haired, sir?" Billy asked eagerly.

Nicholas peered at Freddie's companion, only noticing him now for the first time. "I think she was."

"Did you see her on the day Bertie was drowned?" asked Freddie.

"It might've been, but I can't be sure," Nicholas admitted. "Bertie used to come up here often. It was just when your cousin Marcus came out to work on that motorbike of his, so he might've seen her too. Mind, I didn't hear about Bertie's drowning until he was pulled out of the river, so it may have been a day or two before."

As he and Billy turned away from Nicholas's

cottage, Freddie said, "If Uncle Nick really did see a girl that day, she could very well be the one we're looking for."

"But you don't think it was Miss Celia?" Billy asked. He'd met Celia as a little girl during her visits to Sir Hilliard and still thought of her as "Miss," married or not.

"No, I don't," Freddie said quickly. "Even if she was lying and had been down at the river when Bertie was there, she would've gone straight home afterwards. She'd no reason to come this far up the lane, for Uncle Nick to see her."

"Unless she was running to somebody else. Didn't you say there was another cousin of yours who lives along here?"

"Yes, Agatha. That's her studio, just ahead." Freddie pointed to a cottage on the opposite side of the lane from the two they had just passed: the neatly tended garden was bounded by a low, wooden fence painted white. Red roses climbed trellises on either side of the front door. A sign on the gate that read 'Rose Cottage' was decorated with painted rosebuds around its borders. "But she isn't there now. She's back at the Hall."

"What about her? Has she got dark hair?"

"She does, and so do her sister Amelia and their mother. So do a good many other women." Freddie laughed, a little nervously. "Enough of suspecting my relatives, Billy. If we're not careful, we'll begin to see murderers everywhere!"

9

The George and Dragon Inn was the most prominent building in the Marshbanks high street, with a whitewashed brick facade twice as wide as any of the neighboring shops. Kell's red roadster was parked prominently out front, but when Freddie asked for his cousin, the landlady Mrs. Peabody informed him that "the Capting" wasn't in. His friend Mr. Phillip was, if Freddie wanted to go up.

Freddie and Billy went up to the inn's best room just off the first landing. Before Freddie could knock, the door to the room flew open and Phillip Tollarhithe sprang out. He was a fresh-faced boy of 20 with reddish-brown hair that hadn't been brushed yet that morning and a faint hint of freckles on his nose.

"Freddie, hullo! And Billy, old thing. I knew you'd be coming!" he announced gleefully. "Kell told me he'd set you down at the Hall last night and I've had an eye out the window since I got up, watching for you. Have you had any breakfast?"

"Yes, just before we came out," said Billy.

"Well come in and have some more! I was just sitting down for a bite." Phillip ushered his visitors into the room, where the beds were still unmade and a tea-tray sat on a little table in the bay window overlooking the street. "Shout down the stairs for more cups and hot water, will you, Billy? And ask for more toast if you want some."

"Where's Kell?" asked Freddie while Billy returned to the stair landing to call down to Mrs. Peabody.

"Out," came Phillip's short answer through a gulp of cooling tea. After he'd swallowed, more information followed. "He told you what's been going on? Then you'll understand how he feels. He'd like to get far away from here, but of course he can't go while the police are being such a nuisance and dogging his footsteps. He went out to be by himself as soon as he was up, but you can be sure that detective fellow who's come to town is right behind him. He tries to be discreet, but he's painfully conspicuous in a little place like this. His room's just down the hall. We're still on the Marsh property here, you know. Uncle Win is our landlady's landlord. He could tell her to tell us to pack up and be off at any time—but where can we go?"

"It does sound like precisely the sort of thing that would upset Kell," Freddie said sympathetically as he took a seat at the table across from Phil. He knew how his cousin hated to be bound by restrictions of any kind. "I'd hoped to come and see you both last night, but Uncle Win took me off after dinner for a serious talk about Kell."

"Yes, I heard about that. I saw Dotty, Chubbs, and Bicky down in the bar-parlor last night, and they told me how you were captured by the uncles. But Kell said that was what he'd hoped you'd do."

Freddie was relieved to hear this—not that he'd done as Kell wished, but that the other young men at the Hall had met with Kell and Phillip. They must have deliberately planned it, for there was nowhere else in the village where the two could stay, but there was another pub in Marshbanks, The Landing Lights by the river's edge, where Chubbs and the younger lads could've gone if they'd wanted to avoid the outcasts. It was good to know that his cousin hadn't been entirely shut out by the family.

He said so, and Phillip answered, "Oh, yes, all the lads have rallied 'round. Dotty came by the cottage the morning after Kell's quarrel to say he was on our side, and Chubbs came to call on us right away once he arrived at the Hall. Even old Uncle Nick says he'll stand by Kell... although I don't think he really understands what Kell and I have done to be in trouble. Celia's as sweet as that stick of a husband of hers will let her be, and Agatha had a kind word or two for us when we walked past her place."

"Dotty was there..." Freddie's brow creased in a small, thoughtful frown. Billy returned then, bringing up the hot water and a rack of fresh toast.

"Aunt Emily came by yesterday morning too," Phillip continued as he took a slice of the toast. "She brought some things over for Kell, but I think she wanted to be sure we were all right. She'd have us back at the Hall, but Kell would refuse anyway. And I think I'm better off keeping out of the way 'til this trouble's past." He took a bite of his toast and continued talking through the mouthful. "Not Bertie's murder, I mean. I'm not eager to get in Uncle Winthrop's sight right now. I suppose I'm lucky he hasn't sent me packing off home to Foxgrove in disgrace. Lucky too, that my parents haven't summoned me home. If they did, I'd refuse to go. I won't leave Kell, not while he needs me. I'll sleep under the hedgerows if I have to."

This was the same sort of spirit Phillip had shown at the age of sixteen, when he'd run away from school to London and tried to join the Royal Flying Corp to be with Kell. He had lied about his age but hadn't fooled the recruitment officer, who thought he must be even younger. Phillip's father, Sir Percival Tollarhithe, had to come and take him home. While Freddie thought this sort of thing childishly impulsive and naïve, he couldn't help admiring Phillip's determined sense of loyalty.

"I mean to help Kell too, if I can," he said. "I intend to hunt for whatever facts the police might've overlooked that will prove Kell's innocence. You'll help me, won't you?"

"Yes, of course. What can I do?" Phillip folded his hands on the table and looked attentive and earnest.

"Will you tell me everything that happened that morning? Was there anything odd?"

"It was an odd day even before we knew about Bertie. Kell was upset, you see, by his fight with his father. He'd been tossing all night and he got up early. He didn't touch his breakfast, but he said he was going out. I offered to go with him, but he said he wanted to be by himself and think."

"You stayed at the cottage through the morning?"

Phillip nodded. "I wanted to be there when Kell came back."

"Did you see anyone? Bertie didn't come by, did he?"

"Certainly not."

"What about Dotty? When exactly did he visit?"

"Dotty dropped by around 11:00, but he'd gone by the time Kell came back and we had our lunch. After lunch, Kell said he was sorry he'd been so beastly before, and offered to go out for another walk with me. We went down the lane 'til we got to the river."

"Did you speak to any of your neighbors? Celia? Uncle Nicholas?" asked Freddie.

"Uncle Nick was in his front garden when we went by, but we didn't stop to talk to him. Agatha was clipping her roses and we had a word or two. We didn't see Celia or Marcus."

"Was there a reason you decided to go that particular way?"

"Down the lane? Well... the bar downstairs doesn't open for afternoon business 'til 4:00, and the Landing Lights doesn't even open its door 'til 6:00 when the working men come in. We thought we'd walk along down the river path as slowly as we could and stop in Marshbanks for an ale or two and maybe have our dinner here. Kell was already thinking about taking this room for me and going back to fetch our things from the cottage. But when we found the boat, we went down the path the other way to the Hall boathouse instead to ask them about it. It looked odd to us. The oars were missing."

"You didn't see anyone along the river? Not Bertie, nor anyone else? Any girls?"

"Girls?" Phillip shook his head.

Freddie brought out the swirls of silver from his pocket. "Did you notice this when you discovered Bertie's boat?"

"What is it?" Phillip asked as he took the piece. "It looks like a broken bit of jewelry."

"I found it in the river, near the place where the boat was pulled up onto the bank. It's why I think some girl might've been there. You've never seen it before? You don't know who it belongs to?"

"No," came the regretful answer as Phillip gave it back. "It doesn't look like I've got much useful information for you, does it?"

"Nonsense. You've cleared up several points, and given me one or two ideas to look into. One last question, Phil: You've been at Marsh Hall for weeks. You've seen things first-hand. Do you have any suspicions about who might have wanted to kill Bertie?"

Phillip took another piece of toast and munched thoughtfully. "I've been wondering about that since the police first came to question Kell, but I haven't the least idea. No one liked Bertie—that is, no one who really knew him—but to bash his head in... well, that takes a special kind of hatred, doesn't it? You'd have to want him dead in the worst way to do that. I can't see any of the Marshes getting worked up enough to kill one of their own family and be so vicious about it, not even Kell." Freddie looked shocked, and Phillip explained: "Well, you know it's not true that Kell wouldn't ever kill anybody. He has. He's gotten medals for it."

"Bosch soldiers," Billy said dismissively. "That don't count. When somebody's shooting at you, what else can you do but shoot back and hope you hit 'em first?"

"This wasn't a soldier in battle," said Freddie. "It's a cousin. Even if Kell hated Bertie enough to want to get rid of him—which I don't for a moment believe he did—he wouldn't do it in that ugly and brutal way."

Phillip nodded vigorously. "But how can we tell the police that? They wouldn't understand. They'd only see that if there's one Marsh who's quite good at killing lots of people, it's our Kell."

Footsteps were heard coming up the stairs.

The door to the room had been left open, and Kell appeared on the landing. When he saw the visitors, he smiled.

"Freddie, old chap! What news?"

As Freddie told his cousin about his conversation with Winthrop, the smile vanished.

"I didn't have much hope of you talking Father into reason," said Kell, "but it was worth a try."

"I wish I could've done better for you."

"It isn't your fault. Father won't budge, and that's that." Kell plucked up the last piece of toast from the rack before Billy or Phil claimed it and flopped onto the nearer of the two beds with a sigh. "I've been thinking things over, Freddie. Before the police came to question me, Phil and I were talking over what we'd do if I was disinherited. I thought that we might leave England. Go to America, perhaps. I fancy the idea of New York City. I might look into the aeroplane business. You know I've an interest in flying, and air transport is the future. If I manage to get out of this mess, that's what I'll do. It's the best thing, really. I don't feel as if I belong here anymore. I was a hero in the war, but now I'm only an embarrassment to the family. I'd be better off out of the way. If Bertie was alive, I'd tell him he could be the next Lord Marshbourne and welcome to it. I suppose it'll go to Dotty now. He's next in line."

The other young men exchanged worried glances. Kell was normally so high-spirited and optimistic; they'd never heard him sound bitter like this before.

"You wouldn't be able to get a drink in New York," said Freddie in a gentle attempt at dissuasion.

Kell made a scoffing sound. "I've heard it's easy enough to find, if you know where to go."

"Other things are illegal there as well as here, Kell."

"I don't suppose they'd as make much fuss about that either, not in a city of that size, as long as one wasn't a public disgrace."

"If you went, I couldn't go with you," Phil added, with a pleading note in his voice that suggested he'd said this at least once before. "Father and Mother wouldn't allow it. They never cared much what I did when I was the younger son, but now that Peter's dead, I'm the heir. Suddenly, I'm important. Since I won't come of age 'til October, they can stop me if they want to." He lowered his voice. "They can make all of this much worse for us, Kell."

"It's bad enough as it is," said Kell. "If I must flee the country because of police prying, I'll have to do it right away. Follow me once you turn twenty-one. They can't stop you then, and they won't want to make so much of a fuss that it causes a scandal. Call it a visit and stay on as long as you like."

Phillip shook his head apologetically.

"You shouldn't start your packing just yet, Cap'n," Billy told Kell. "We're working on something that'll give the police somebody else to think about."

"What's that?" Kell sat up and stared at Billy, then turned to Freddie. "What're you planning to do?"

"I've decided to conduct my own investigation," Freddie explained. "I doubt I can solve Bertie's murder for the police, but I hope to turn their attention elsewhere before they pry too deeply into your private life."

This news made Kell laugh. "Find the murderer or not, you're certain to do a better job than the police, old thing. You couldn't help it—you're more clever than the whole lot of them together."

"I believe that by focusing their attention on you, they've missed some important clues that point in another direction entirely," Freddie went on.

Now, Kell was intensely interested. "Really? Who do you think did it?"

"Well, it's only a theory of mine," Freddie answered, curbing his enthusiasm; he didn't want to give Kell false hopes. "Billy and I have found some signs there's a girl involved—a girl who was in the boat with Bertie that day. I've been down to the river this morning to have a look at the spot where you and Phillip found the boat, and I discovered this." He took the broken ornament from his pocket.

Kell reached out to take it, turned it over in his fingers to examine it. His expression, which had been avid only seconds before, suddenly went blank. "This was down by the river, you say?"

"Yes, in the rushes. Do you have any idea who might've lost it there?"

"No, I've never seen it before." Kell tossed the trinket back to Freddie.

"It doesn't belong to anyone you know?"

"Not that I know of. Sorry, Freddie. I wish I could say otherwise, but I can't."

Kell was a good liar when he needed to be, but Freddie knew him too well to be fooled; he could see that his cousin was keeping something back.

∗∗∗

"He won't go," Billy declared in an undertone after they'd left Phil and Kell and were heading downstairs a short while later.

"I believe he might," answered Freddie. "He's got enough of an incentive, between this trouble with the police and his quarrel with his father. Besides, he's been restless and unhappy since the war ended and hasn't even had the trouble of his wounds to occupy him, since he never had any. He's been kept idle since he came home, and he isn't by nature an idler. He wants something to do."

"Wish I had such troubles," said Billy, and Freddie turned to him at the foot of the stair.

"You don't like Kell, do you, Billy?"

"He gets at me, that's all. That toff pose of his. If I hear him say 'old thing' one more time, there's going to be another murder done."

This made Freddie laugh.

"Now, what about the way Cap'n Kell–"

Freddie swiftly raised a hand for silence. As they were about to cross the inn's public room to reach the front door, he saw that they weren't alone. A man was seated at a table in the otherwise empty bar. It was too early in the day for a drink; Mrs. Peabody had brought him a cup of coffee and he was smoking a cigarette as he read the local newspaper. His trench coat lay thrown over the seat beside him. There was a hard look to his face, remarkable even in these post-war times when plenty of younger men had been hardened. He couldn't be mistaken for a Marshbanks man, a tourist, or even a commercial traveler. Phil was quite right; he was conspicuous.

The man looked up suddenly from his newspaper. Freddie had the feeling that he'd been waiting for them to return from Kell's room.

"You're the police detective," he said, determined not to be intimidated.

"Inspector John Deffords, Norfolk Constabulary," the man introduced himself.

"They sent you from Wymondham to investigate the murder of Bertram Marsh?"

"Yes, that's right. And you are..?"

"Frederick Babington. This is my servant, William Watkins." Billy stood at his elbow, regarding the policeman warily.

"Babington?" Deffords repeated the name. Freddie thought he intended to write it down in those little notebooks that policemen always carried with them in mystery stories, but the inspector said, "There's a famous scholar of antiquities and civilizations of the Middle East named Sir Hilliard Babington. A great traveler too, in his day. He was in Khartoum when General Gordon was killed."

"My uncle," said Freddie. "Are you acquainted with him?" He felt as if the inspector had offered him a letter of recommendation, and at the same time felt a sense of relief that annoyed him. It wasn't a rational feeling, he knew, but an inescapable prejudice of his class that people who knew your people must be all right.

"I haven't had the pleasure of meeting Sir Hilliard personally," Deffords answered. "I worked in Intelligence in Cairo during the war. Your uncle provided information about the Arabs that was of great help to us in dealing with them."

Freddie nodded. He knew that his uncle

had done that sort of war work, though Hilliard had never confided the particulars to him.

"You're a friend of Captain Marsh?" Deffords asked him.

"We're cousins, actually. Lord Marshbourne is also my uncle, on the other side. My mother was his half-sister and my father was the famous Sir Hilliard's younger brother Douglas. You won't have heard of him. They both died when I was a child. Lord and Lady Marshbourne brought me up."

"You must've also known the murdered boy Bertram?"

"Yes, quite well. We all grew up together." Feeling bolder, Freddie ventured, "You've been through the war yourself, Inspector. You know how it was. Surely, you understand that just because he's killed men during the war, that doesn't mean that Kell would murder our cousin in cold blood."

"Has Captain Marsh killed many men?" Deffords looked almost amused.

"He was a highly decorated pilot during the war. A hero. I'd hate to think that his bravery was being used against him now."

"It isn't," Defford told him. "I remember how it was during the war. I shot men myself, though nobody gave me medals for it. A lot of men can say the same." Billy gave a solemn nod, and the inspector's eyes flickered briefly to him before they returned to Freddie. "What about you, Mr. Babington—or is it Captain Babington?

"No, I was only a lieutenant. I haven't used it since. I'm afraid I can't claim any dead men or medals for my service, only some scars that have taken a long time to heal."

"Your cousin's younger than you, isn't he?"

"Yes, by nearly two years." Freddie felt that the inspector was prodding him for some sign of jealousy or resentment. "I don't begrudge Kell his successes. I'm quite proud of him. He's always been like a brother to me, and I mean to stand by him as long as he's under suspicion. It's only right that I tell you frankly—I mean to prove he didn't do this."

Deffords's eyebrows went up at this announcement. "Are you a detective yourself, Mr. Babington?"

"No," Freddie admitted, "but I've read books."

"Sherlock Holmes? The police in those detective stories are always bumbling idiots."

"Not always. In the one I'm reading now, the chap from Scotland Yard is no fool. He and the private detective are the best of friends." It occurred to him as he spoke that there was another policeman in the novel who was exactly that sort of idiot, but he refrained from mentioning it. "I won't make that mistake, Inspector, but I have advantages in this case that the police don't. I know the people involved intimately. You simply don't know Kell as I do. I realize that my belief in his innocence isn't enough to convince you of anything, so I must find some proof. If I do, I won't hesitate to bring it to you."

"I'd appreciate it if you did, Mr. Babington, but you ought to be careful." The inspector spoke gravely, but Freddie still suspected that he was amused. The man couldn't be more than 10 or 12 years older than he was, but made him feel like a callow and stupid boy. "Investigations of real murders are dangerous. If you're right and Captain Marsh is innocent, the person who killed Bertram Marsh might resent your prying. He wouldn't hesitate to make you his second victim if you found some evidence against him."

Freddie had opened his mouth to reply, when the street door opened and Marshbank's Constable Hobart entered the inn. He was a local man who had kept the peace in the neighborhood surrounding Marsh Hall for years, capable of dealing with drunken fishermen and the occasional petty theft, but Freddie had no doubt that he was in over his head with murder. If there was a bumbling policeman in this case, then Hobart was a better candidate than the man sent specially to investigate Bertie's death.

Hobart immediately noticed Freddie. "Why, if it isn't Mr. Freddie! Good to see you home again, lad, though it's a pity it couldn't be for happier reasons. Been to see Mr. Kell—Capting Kell, I oughter say?"

Freddie acknowledged that he'd just seen his cousin. "You've known Kell from a boy, Hobbie. Surely you don't really think he murdered Bertie, do you?"

"I don't like to, Mr. Freddie, but there are things that don't look right and we can't pretend they do just 'cause he's His Lordship's own son. Even His Lordship says that's so. But we called in the inspector here. Did you meet Inspector Deffords? Ah, you did. Then you know he's looking into it?"

"I'd like to hear more about your investigation." Freddie turned from Hobart to the inspector to address them both. "Do you have other suspects beyond Kell? You must have looked, or else you'd have arrested him by now."

"I'm asking them as live in Marshbanks and 'round the Hall if they've seen any strangers or suspicious characters lurking about," Hobart replied. "I just come to report to the inspector about it." He brandished a notebook.

"Have you spoken to the people at the Hall? Not just the family, but the servants? There may be something there you've missed."

"I interviewed the viscount's family as well as the servants at Marsh Hall," Deffords replied.

"When you first arrived? Have you been back since?"

"We don't wish to disturb His Lordship nor any of his household more'n is necessary 'til we have some news to report," said Hobart.

"And have you any?"

Hobart shook his head.

"Have you been back to the spot where Bertie's boat was left? Have you asked the members of the family that live in the lane if they saw anybody near the river that day?"

"I did just after Mr. Bertram was taken out of the river, but they didn't have much to say."

"Perhaps you ought to talk to them again," Freddie suggested. "My cousin Cecilia tells me that she didn't see Kell go toward the riverside that morning around the time Bertie must've been there." Billy was giving him a quizzical glance; Freddie put one hand into his coat pocket but didn't bring out its contents.

"I'm sorry, but that don't mean a thing one way or another," Hobart responded. He had begun to huff at these persistent questions, but now he added in more conciliatory tones, "Now, don't you worry, Mr. Freddie. If Mr. Kell's innocent, we'll turn something up and it'll come out right in the end. Just you leave us to do our investigating as we see fit."

Deffords had said little, but continued to observe Freddie during this conversation with Hobart. Now he spoke, "If you want to help your cousin, Mr. Babington, you won't mind answering a few questions about him."

"Not at all," said Freddie, "but you must know that I wasn't here when Bertie was killed. I only arrived on the London train yesterday afternoon."

The inspector waved this aside. "What I want to know is what is it that Captain Marsh and Lord Marshbourne won't tell me about their quarrel."

Freddie was caught off guard by this question that went straight to the heart of what they were trying to hide. "I– I'm afraid I don't know," he answered.

"Don't you? Even though you and the Captain are like brothers?"

"We are, but he doesn't tell me everything."

Deffords didn't look as if he believed it, but he only said, "I'm sorry to hear that. I think that if I knew what'd happened between them during that fight, it might make a deal of difference in the case against your cousin."

"Yes, I'm certain it would, Inspector," Freddie agreed, "but there's nothing I can say about it."

✳✳✳

11

"I thought you were going to tell them about that girl in the boat and the piece of jewelry you found?" Billy said once they had left the inn and were out on the street.

"I meant to," Freddie admitted, "but they wouldn't care about it. The story about the girl is just that—a story, no more. The girl Uncle Nick saw might be anybody, or she might've been there on another day. I need to find something more substantial. Until I do, I'm only a foolish meddler. You heard how stuffy Constable Hobart became because I asked him a few questions. And that policeman from Wymondham would only laugh to himself at my playing detective. I'd rather keep out of his way as much as I can. He is no fool and I've a feeling he isn't done with me and Kell's quarrel with Uncle Win yet. As for this- ah- clue of ours," he patted his pocket, "I'd better hold onto it awhile longer, 'til I learn more about it. I don't know if it has anything to do with Bertie's death, but it does mean something to Kell."

"He was lying," Billy murmured under his breath.

"I know. Kell knows who that trinket belongs to, but why won't he tell me?" That was what stung the most. "I'm trying to help him. Doesn't he see that?" Then Freddie stopped in the street and gripped Billy's arm. "Bill, it must be someone at the Hall! Kell's trying to protect her. One of the family? Yes, that's the only answer that makes sense. Kell would speak up if it were anyone else. A cousin? One of the aunties? Surely not his mother." He shook his head. "I can't see Aunt Emily smashing anyone's head in. It's too absurd. In fact, none of the ladies at the Hall, even the dark-haired ones, seem likely as a murderess." He spoke as if he were joking, but a serious, unpleasant idea was forming in his mind: what if the broken piece of jewelry were Celia's and she had lied about it? Would Kell lie for her? "When we get back to the Hall, I'll have to find out."

"Not right off, you're not," Billy said with a no-nonsense tone. "You've done your running about for the morning. You'll've walked more'n a mile by the time we're back at Marsh Hall and you said you'd rest for a bit before the funeral. You can do more investigating afterwards."

"I'll rest," Freddie promised. He was beginning to feel weary after his morning's exertions. "But you must work for me while I'm resting. Be my eyes and ears, remember?"

Billy nodded. "What d'you want me to do?"

"The servants won't attend the funeral. It'll be the perfect time for you to ask them some questions."

"Do you want me to show that bit of jewelry about?"

"No, I'll do that myself among the family. I'd rather not have very many people know about it before I know who it belongs to. But there are a few other things I'd like to find out more about. If we're going to conduct our own investigation properly, we must be methodical and go through every step in an orderly fashion." He enumerated the questions he wanted answers to, counting them off on his fingers: "First, we have to determine for a fact if Bertie was alone or if he had someone with him when he went out—and if there was, who she was. I'd also like to know exactly when he left, and if he said anything about where he was going. The men who work at the Hall boathouse will be able to tell you that. The boathouse is that big, wooden building that hangs out over the river at the southernmost end of the garden. If you follow the path under the willows along the river's edge, you can't help but find your way to it. Second, I want to know where Dotty was. Ask the boatsmen about him as well. They can tell you when he went out and when he came back." He told Billy, "Last night at dinner, Dotty said that he'd been fishing at the Upper Lock pool that morning, but that's not where he went, not if he was visiting Phil at Thicket Cottage. You heard Phil say so."

Billy nodded. "I saw how you took particular note of that, but I couldn't see why. You don't think he's the one?"

"I don't know! I don't want to think anything so horrible about a cousin of mine, but I know he lied. It's hardly possible for him to have been in both places—the two are miles apart. I think that he must've taken a boat, so that he could say he was going south to Upper Lock when he rowed downriver instead... perhaps to follow Bertie."

"Why'd he do that?"

Freddie voiced his worst thoughts: "What if this piece of jewelry belongs to Celia? What if she did go to the river to meet Bertie, and someone else followed and found them there?"

"But why Mr. Daed'lus, not her husband?" Billy looked confused.

"Yes, I thought it might be Marcus, at first— but, Billy, Dotty is Celia's brother." He could see Billy's expression brighten with understanding.

"He wouldn't like it any better than her husband would."

Freddie tried to imagine what had happened: Bertie had stopped at the landing at the end of the lane for a pre-arranged meeting with Celia. Dotty had known about it and followed him there in a second boat, and surprised the two in their tryst. To avenge his sister's honor, he'd struck Bertie, knocking him into the river deliberately or by accident—and then what? Could he have gone to pay a friendly visit to Phillip after committing this murderous assault? Phillip wasn't the most observant boy but surely he would have noticed if Dotty were behaving oddly. And what about Celia? If she had witnessed Dotty's fight with Bertie, that might explain why she'd run up the lane past Uncle Nicholas's cottage instead of going home; she was seeking help or shelter from Agatha. But if she'd seen the two fighting, she must also know or guess that her brother was responsible for Bertie's death. She might lie to protect him, but would she be so composed about it? Celia had seemed upset about Bertie when Freddie had spoken to her, but not as upset as a girl whose brother had murdered her lover might reasonably be.

It didn't make sense. Something wasn't right.

"No." He stopped himself. "I mustn't jump to conclusions before I have the facts. I need to know more. Ask about Dotty, and you might try to find out if there was any gossip about Celia and Bertie, before or after her marriage."

Billy nodded.

"I doubt if you'll be able to learn what the family in the lane were all doing, but can you find out who else was away from the Hall that morning?"

Freddie counted off a third finger. "After Dotty told us where he was supposed to have been, some of the others at the table told where they were as well." He tried to remember. "Chubbs said he wasn't here yet. Amelia said she'd gone out for a walk. Perhaps someone can tell us where she went. Bicky said he slept late. That one might be easiest to discover the truth of. Whatever you find, you can tell me about it after the funeral."

12

As he entered Marsh Hall through one of the garden front doors, Freddie was intercepted by Winthrop. His uncle must have been watching for him from the study windows, for Winthrop appeared at the door to his room almost immediately. "If you don't mind, Frederick lad—a word or two before lunch?"

"Yes, Uncle, of course." With a glance at Billy, who nodded and went up the back stairs, Freddie went into the study. He was relieved to see that Uncle Kellynch was not there; he knew that Uncle Winthrop meant to ask him about Kell, and it would be much easier for them to talk without those poisonous asides.

Winthrop shut the study door. "You've been to Marshbanks?" he asked. "Had your talk with Kell?"

"I've spoken with him," Freddie answered.

"And will he see reason?"

"If you mean does Kell intend break with Phillip, Uncle, then the answer is no. He refuses to do so." When Winthrop's mouth turned down in a disappointed frown, Freddie added quickly, "As a matter of fact, he spoke of leaving for America rather than agree to that."

"Leave England?" To Winthrop Marsh, such a thing was unimaginable.

"That is what Kell said," Freddie confirmed. "He spoke of New York City and the aeroplane business. He won't change his mind, but he doesn't wish to be an embarrassment to the family." He believed that Kell had spoken in despair and anger, but also thought that Winthrop ought to see how strongly his son felt about this intolerable situation.

This had the effect on Winthrop that Freddie hoped it would. "He doesn't have to do that!"

"Can you blame him for feeling that way about it, Uncle Win?"

"Oh, I know the boy feels he's in a tight spot, but that's no reason to do anything rash. If he'd just sit still another day or two, be patient until the police have investigated the matter fully and cleared him, then everything will be all right. And I do blame Kell for getting himself into this." The viscount paced the room. "If only he'd be sensible, marry a nice girl, and do his duty to the family. That's all I ask. I wouldn't even care what he and Phil Tollarhithe got up to in private if he'd behave himself in public. None of this would've happened if he'd just done that."

"Bertie wouldn't have been killed?" Freddie asked, puzzled.

"No, I didn't mean that. If Kell had done as I'd asked, we would never have quarreled. No suspicion would've fallen on him when poor Bertie died and I wouldn't be in the absurd position of seeing my own son—the next Lord Marshbourne!—

questioned by the police for his cousin's murder. I wouldn't have put Bertie in his place, not really," Winthrop grudgingly confessed. "Bertie was a fine lad but he never had Kell's cleverness, if Kell only would put his wits to good use."

"Perhaps if you'd told Kell–" Freddie began, when there was a tentative knock on the study door. The family and guests who were there for the funeral were waiting to go into lunch, but couldn't sit down to eat until the master of the house was there to preside over the table.

The same party was at lunch as had been at dinner the night before, with the additions of the newly married couple returned from their cottage and Agatha, who sat red-eyed beside her younger sister Amelia. Agatha Marsh was a tall woman of twenty-eight, of a somber disposition even at the best of times. Where Amelia embraced the modern age, Agatha, like Marcus, seemed to belong to the Victorian era—but to the artistic rather than the prim and straight-laced aspect of that earlier time. In her long, black dress with plaits of dark hair along either side of her angular-but-arresting face, Freddie thought that she looked like a suitable companion for Christina Rossetti or a model for one of Dante Gabriel Rossetti's paintings.

"Have the final arrangements been made for this afternoon?" asked Aunt Beatrice. "Are we quite ready to see poor Bertie to his rest?"

"Nearly so," said Emily, "but we need another boy to help as pallbearer." By long-standing tradition, young men of the Marsh family carried the coffin into the church and, after the service, into the vault beneath it.

"It ought to be a son of the house," Dotty said pointedly, "but we seem to be short of them these days."

"There aren't enough suitable youths," Emily agreed more tactfully, "but Charles has been kind enough to volunteer and I hope we can ask Emeric Marsh's sons to help when their family arrives. Sarah telephoned this morning to say that they will be motoring over from Acre House. I was hoping, Freddie, that you might stand in for Kell at the ceremony." Kell wasn't expected to attend the funeral. "Are you feeling quite well enough for the duty?"

"I'd be glad to, Aunt Emily." Freddie tried to recall exactly what the heir was required to do on these occasions. The last family funeral he'd attended had been his grandfather's. That had been a very large and grand affair, with gentry from all over England turning out to pay their respects to Viscount Roderick of Marshbourne; today's funeral, by contrast, would be a much smaller and more private ceremony. He'd only been eight at the time, and Kell six; they had only been required to sit still. "I won't have to give a speech, will I?" The memorial speeches for the last Lord Marshbourne had gone on for hours.

"Only if you'd like to, dear," his aunt assured him. "Otherwise, you have only to lead the procession into the church and stand beside poor Bertie's coffin during the service and farewells. Who is going to speak? Kellynch, you will, certainly."

"Yes, of course," said Kellynch. "And you, Win? You were fond of my boy—that's only fitting."

"I'd like to say my farewells," said Beatrice,

"just as I did for my poor sister, his mother. I never thought I would outlive them both."

"What about you, Agatha dear?" Emily addressed her eldest niece with tender solicitude. "Do you feel fit to attend the funeral? Would you like to say a few words about Bertie?"

Agatha nodded. "I will be present, Auntie," she answered. She reached to take her sister's hand, and Amelia gave her fingers a comforting squeeze.

13

After lunch, Freddie approached the two sisters as they left the table. "Aggie, Mellie. May I talk to you?"

"We were just going up to our rooms," said Amelia. "Agatha ought to rest."

"Yes," Agatha agreed. "I need to lie down for awhile... before we go over to the church."

"I'm going to rest too." Freddie smiled softly. "I promised I would." The pair didn't object as he left the dining hall and went up the stairs with them. "Do you mind?" he asked. "I'm trying to help Kell. I'd like to ask you both a question or two about the day Bertie died."

Agatha gripped her sister's arm. "What do you want to know?"

"I wanted to ask about Celia."

"Celia?" Agatha echoed. Both sisters looked puzzled.

"She didn't pay a call on you, did she?"

"No," said Agatha. "I didn't see Celia that day. Only Mellie."

"Mellie?" Freddie was surprised. "Is that where you were going?" he asked Amelia. "You said last night you were out for a walk. You went to Agatha's?"

"Yes, if you must know," the younger woman answered. "I went to visit my sister. I spent the day at Rose Cottage, and we walked back to the Hall together for dinner."

Freddie wondered if she was the dark-haired girl Nicholas had seen, and not Cecilia. "Did you notice if Uncle Nicholas was out in his garden when you passed, Mellie?"

"Uncle Nick? No, I didn't notice him." Amelia cast a glance at her sister. "Was he there?"

"He said he saw a girl go past his cottage," Freddie explained. "I thought it was Celia, but I'm afraid Uncle Nick doesn't see all that well any more." He felt rather silly; he'd been imagining a girl flying down the lane in fright, when all the time it had been Mellie going on an ordinary visit. This was what came of jumping to conclusions and letting his imagination mislead him.

"Here, Freddie," Marcus called out. Freddie stopped, but Agatha and Amelia took the opportunity to go on alone. Because of his damaged knee, Marcus didn't come up after his cousin, but continued to speak loudly from the foot of the stairs. "What d'you mean by going around asking everybody questions?" he demanded. "Well, no more! I won't have it. You've upset my wife, and now you're making a nuisance of yourself to my sisters. What is it you're after?"

"Whatever proof I can find that Kell didn't kill Bertie," Freddie responded frankly. "I don't wish to distress the girls more than they've already been distressed by this, but if they can tell me anything that will help to keep Kell from the danger of being arrested, then I will ask them. I want to see justice done, don't you?"

Marcus grudgingly admitted that he wanted justice, even if he didn't approve of Kell. "But just you mind, Freddie Babington—don't go bothering them any more than you have to. I'll put a stop to it if you don't, Kell be hanged or not!"

When Freddie went to his room for his nap, he found Billy placing his clothes for the funeral over the back of a chair. Freddie sat down on the bed and told Billy about his latest conversation with his uncle as he took off his coat and the sweater-vest he wore beneath it.

"You think His Lordship'll come around after all?" Billy asked as he took the cast-off garments and put them in the wardrobe.

"I don't know yet, but I've given him something to think about." Freddie slipped his braces off his shoulders and lay down. "Uncle Win isn't so bad, usually. He's not the warmest-hearted man, but he's always had a strong sense of family honor. His behavior of late hasn't been the best, but that's only because he's so proud. Uncle Win's put it all on Kell to carry on the ancient Marsh line, but for the same reason, he wouldn't set his only son aside. It'd be too great a wound to his pride. He'll threaten Kell with disinheritance, but he says now that he never really meant to put Bertie in Kell's place. I wonder if Bertie knew that, or if he thought Uncle Win actually meant to do it?" He sighed and looked up as Billy came to stand beside the bed. "Did you get any answers to my questions in the servants' hall?"

"There wasn't any proper lunch today, as

they had the 'freshments for after the funeral to get ready and the rest of the maids were out in the yard with the laundry," Billy reported. "But while I was having a bite to eat in the kitchen, I got on good terms with some of the older servants. That's mostly due to you."

"To me?"

"The ones that remember when you was a boy here have naught but good things to say of you. Old Brambley hears tell you've gone a mite peculiar since you come back from the war, but he's sure you've kept a sound head in spite of it."

Freddie laughed.

"If I wanted stories about what you were like as a little lad growing up," said Billy, "I could get more'n enough to suit. They'll tell me anything about the Marshes if I ask."

"Have they told you anything?"

"I heard a bit more about Mr. Bertram's carryings-on. I asked 'em about Miss Cecilia. She ran a bit wild, they say, when she was still a miss. She went off with Mr. Bertram from time to time after she got home from her school last summer, and there was other boys when she was in London. Them in the servants' hall had it that she was to marry Mr. Bertie once she was of an age, but then she wed Mr. Marcus instead, him being more steady-like. After that, Mr. Bertram started courting one of your other cousins."

"Agatha," guessed Freddie. Upon reflection, it seemed obvious: Agatha had been too upset to come down to dinner last night, and why else would Aunt Emily invite her in particular to speak over Bertie unless there was a special connection between them? "Is there more?"

"I'll be going to the boathouse while you're off at the funeral, and I'll to talk to the housemaids when they come in. They'll know the most about the family's comings and goings."

"Is that what you're going to do next?"

"Just as soon as I see you resting." Billy drew the curtains over the windows. "Go to sleep."

Freddie was glad to comply. He did feel very tired, almost as if it were an effort to keep his eyes open. He shut them.

Just before he dropped off, he heard a light tap on the door. Billy opened it, and spoke softly: "Can you come back later, Effie? Mr. Fred'rick's sleeping and mustn't be disturbed. Wait, I've got a question for you." Then he went out into the hallway.

14

"It doesn't matter about Mr. Freddie's bed," said the maid named Effie as she and Billy went into the room next door. "He only slept in his sheets the one night, and we'll get 'em for washing after you've gone." As she began to strip the bed, she glanced up at Billy and asked, "Will you be staying with us for very long?"

"I don't know rightly," Billy answered, and came forward to help her gather up the bundle of sheets. "We'll stay 'til we've finished what we came here for." He looked about the bedroom, which was very like the one Freddie was staying in, but slightly smaller and without an adjacent dressing-room. "Whose room is this?"

"Mr. Charles Burke, who's visiting too."

"He didn't come 'til just before we did,"

Billy recalled. "Isn't that so?"

"Yes, that's right. Just the day before." As they left the room, Effie took the armload of sheets from Billy and dropped them into a large wicker basket sitting in the hallway. "He's come up for the funeral. But his sister Miss Louisa's been here awhile with their aunt. This is her room," she announced as they went into another room farther along the passage. "A sweet little miss, she is, and hardly any trouble to look after, 'cept for that once..."

As they went from room to room, Billy helping the maid gather the bed-sheets, she told him many interesting things about the occupants of each. Billy listened attentively, asked questions, and thought he would never be able to remember it all to tell Freddie. He'd have to write everything down when he got a chance.

"You're sweet to give a hand, Bill Watkins," Effie told him when they'd finished with the last bedroom. "It's got my job done so much quicker."

"Glad to've helped," Billy mumbled rather shyly. It was the least he could do to repay her for the information she'd given him. He had only one question left to ask. "Can you tell me, Eff? We've been in all the rooms. Which one belonged to this Mr. Bertram who died?"

"It's that one." Effie pointed to a closed door at the far end of the hallway, a room they hadn't entered. "It's been shut up. Naught to look at, if you've a mind to go in. Why d'you want to?"

"Oh, just curious. I've heard so much talk about him. All sorts of odd things."

"That's no surprise," she laughed. "Mr. Bertie was a caution! Mr. Brambley warned me about 'm the day I started to work here. 'You're a pretty girl,' he said. 'Watch yourself 'round that one.'"

Billy wondered if Bertram Marsh had paid improper attention to Effie—she was quite pretty—but he couldn't suspect her. They were looking for a dark-haired girl, and Effie's was yellow. "He didn't give you any trouble, did he?"

The question made Effie smile at him. "No," she answered, "save for a teasing word or two. I was on my guard, but I heard stories about girls that wasn't." She leaned closer to Billy and told him confidentially, "Last summer, there was a maid who worked here, Milly, her name was. She had to go off and marry quick-like to a lad at one of the farms down the river. She had her baby only three months after." Her eyes were wide. "Now that's scandal enough, but 'twas settled right enough in the end, 'til her husband came to the Hall wanting to see Mr. Bertie- wanting to fight him over Milly. He said Mr. Bertie'd disgraced her."

Billy was agog at the dazzling array of sexual indiscretions he'd discovered going on around Marsh Hall—and all centered around one person! "You mean the baby was Mr. Bertie's?" he whispered.

"Well, there's no way of knowing," Effie admitted. "Cook has it that even Milly wouldn't know one way or the other. But her husband wouldn't have any more to do with her after that. She and the baby went home to her family and been living there since. What else can we think?"

Billy agreed that this was suggestive. "What about the husband? Did he fight Mr. Bertram?"

"No," the girl answered regretfully. "Mr.

Brambley sent him off, and he never saw Mr. Bertie."

Billy was eager to find out more about this incident, but before he could ask for more details, there was a shout from someone below, "Eff!"

"Coming!" Effie shouted back, and gave Billy another smile. "I shouldn't stand here a-talking all day when there's work to be done." She shoved the contents of the wicker basket down a chute beside the narrow back stairs used by the servants, tossed the basket into a nearby closet, and went down the stairs.

After she'd gone, Billy tried the door to Bertie's room, and found it locked.

15

When Freddie woke from his nap, Billy hadn't returned. Still out asking questions, Freddie concluded. Since his clothes had been laid out for him, he had only to wash and dress before the funeral.

He went down to the back parlor where Bertie's body had been laid out. The other pallbearers stood waiting outside the door: Dotty, Bicky, Chubbs, and two distant Marsh cousins, Marmaduke and Eustace, who were also in their early twenties.

"I'm sorry," Freddie said as he joined them. "Am I late?"

"No," Chubbs assured him. "We're waiting for Uncle Win to let us into the parlor. The door's locked."

"It's good of you to give a hand, Freddie," said Dotty. "I say, are you sure you're feeling up to it?"

"The doctors tell me there's very little wrong with me physically any more," Freddie answered. "The burn scars on my hand will fade. My leg just needs some exercise to put it right."

"Well, this will certain give you some exercise, old chap," said Bicky. "And if you feel a little weak, Chubbs can take up that end for you. He could probably carry the whole weight of the thing over one shoulder."

"Even if Kell were here, it'd be impossible for him to do this," said Chubbs. "The way Uncle Kellynch feels, he'd throttle him barehanded if he dared to touch Bertie's coffin."

"And Aunt Emily couldn't possibly ask Phil to take the duty," added Dotty. "I hope they have the sense not to show up. This funeral's going to be awkward as it is."

"Imagine if they did come," said Eustace. He and his brother had evidently heard all the family gossip.

They fell quiet as Winthrop Marsh and Brambley arrived. The butler brought out a large ring of keys from his waistcoat pocket and unlocked the parlor door.

"Ready, lads? It's time," Winthrop said as the door was opened. "The family cars are being brought 'round to the front, but I've asked the undertaker to bring his coach to this side of the house. The garden door has already been opened. Once you've brought poor Bertie out and seen him into the coach, come and join us at the front. You'll all go together in the second car behind the coach, and be out of it and ready to carry him into the church."

With a chorus of "Yes, Uncle," the young

men followed Lord Marshbourne into the darkened parlor, lit only by shafts of sunlight that filtered in through the gaps between the closed curtains and the crack of the slightly ajar outer door. The coffin sat on trestles at the center of the room; Freddie was surprised to see that the lid was closed.

They each took a brass handle and lifted the coffin, taking care not to let it tip. Brambley held the garden door open for them, and the undertaker's men were ready to help them place it in the glass-sided coach festooned with black crepe and drawn by black horses with plumed headdresses waiting outside. Once the coach began to move, the six young men went around to the front of the Hall, where several ponderous black automobiles were waiting. The viscount and viscountess were already seated in the back of their pre-war Royce with Kellynch and Aunt Beatrice. A driver stood waiting at the open passenger door of the second, a new Lanchester; the pallbearers climbed in. Once the funeral coach had gone past, they followed at what seemed like a snail's pace toward the church. Vehicles containing the rest of the family and the neighboring gentry who had come to attend the funeral fell in behind, forming a procession.

"They couldn't show Bertie," Dotty told Freddie. "That's why the coffin's closed and the parlor door was kept locked. He's not a pretty sight. He was in the water, you know, for two days before they fished him out."

"Did you see him?" Eustace asked eagerly.

"No." Dotty shook his head. "No one's been allowed to view him since he's been laid out, except for the undertaker."

"Lou told me that Aunt Beatrice wanted to see him when the men first brought him back to the Hall," Chubbs added. "Uncle Winthrop told her she'd better not."

"It's more than Bertie's being in the water for so long, isn't it?" asked Marmaduke. "We've heard that his head was dreadfully bashed in when they found him."

"That's true," said Bicky. "That's how old Hobbie knew it wasn't an accident and called in the Constabulary right away, although why they lit on Kell..."

The car stopped; they were at the church.

St. Botolph's-on-the-Marshland sat at a slightly elevated position of prominence above the flat and once-marshy lands surrounding it, just beyond Marsh Hall's northern gate and a short walk from the village of Marshbanks. A church had stood on this spot since 1100, but the present building was no more than 100 years old; in the Victorian gothic revivalist style, it looked more medieval than the 17th-century structure it had replaced. The vaults beneath it were much older. The rectory, a large and rambling Victorian building, sat behind the church, half-concealed by tall trees. Its only inhabitants at present were Dr. Grant, Aunt Matilda's father, and his elderly housekeeper. Matilda and her children had never lived there and didn't expect to as long as Stephen Marsh preferred the Hall.

Dr. Grant performed the funeral service, as he had performed every Sunday service, wedding, funeral, and christening in the parish for over fifty years. He spoke of how the Marsh family must sorrow over the death of so promising a young man, but made no mention of how Bertie had died. He seemed certain that the young man's soul had found a place in Heaven. Beatrice wept openly. Celia's eyes brimmed with tears and she hid her nose in her handkerchief. At the back of the church stood Nicholas, still in his old tweeds and looking impatient. Inspector Deffords also sat at the back, less conspicuous here among so many people although he wasn't wearing black.

Once the service concluded and the organ began to play, Freddie stepped forward to lead the pallbearers to the coffin. They lifted it again and bore it carefully along the aisle and down the worn steps into the ancient vault beneath the church. Gas lanterns had been placed in the antechamber below before the ceremony and a wooden platform stood near the foot of the steps. The pallbearers placed the coffin here and stood ranged on one side, their heads bowed and hands clasped respectfully while those who wished to said a few words of remembrance for Bertie. In accordance with family custom, mourners could bid farewell to the departed before he was taken to his final resting place within the crypt.

Most of the people who'd attended the service above didn't come below for this final part of the ceremony, for the antechamber wasn't large and the stone archways leading away into the darkness of the burial vaults were rather spooky. Though the oldest stone facings had been defaced or worn into illegibility over the centuries, the Marshes, Marishes, and de Mariscos of many generations still lay here. Cromwell's men had set fire to the old church, but the crypt had suffered only minor vandalism at their hands.

Lord Marshbourne spoke first, praising his nephew and lamenting his loss. Kellynch spoke next, showing more anger than grief as he vowed justice for his murdered son. Others followed, those who had known Bertie and wished to remember him fondly. A sympathetic hush fell over the group when Agatha stepped forward to place a bunch of flowers upon the coffin. She turned to face the gathered mourners as if she meant to speak, but only burst into tears.

"Poor Agatha's all torn up about Bertie," Dotty murmured as the young woman quickly swept up the steps into the church. From where the pallbearers stood, they could see her sink down into the pew nearest the altar and sob into her handkerchief. Amelia followed her sister upstairs and stood over her, offering comforting whispers and pats; Theresa joined them. "Except for Uncle Kell, this must be most distressing for her. There was an understanding between the two of them, you know."

"No, I hadn't heard." But it confirmed Freddie's guess.

After this, only a few more mourners came forward to say their farewells. Once the last had finished, Winthrop gave a solemn nod and the pallbearers, taking this cue, resumed their places around the coffin and lifted it one last time. The church sexton and the undertaker had prepared an empty shelf not far from the vault entrance for them; the sexton took up one of the lanterns and led them to it

"Not room for many more Marshes down here," he said with a grim humor. "His Lordship'll have to see about having a new vault dug out if he means the family to carry on."

Bertie's coffin was placed upon its shelf. A memorial slab would be added to cover the opening, as the other Marsh coffins lay concealed.

As the group emerged from the vault, they could hear Agatha still sobbing. "Bertie—*why*?" in spite of her mother's and sister's efforts to comfort her. At last, Amelia and Theresa quietly escorted her out of the church.

16

"That wasn't as awful as I thought it'd be," Chubbs said as the pallbearers walked back to the Hall together. It was a pleasant spring day and not a long walk through the Hall park. None of them wanted to crowd into the Lanchester after being in the crypt. "Except for poor Agatha."

"I thought it was Celia who'd cry over Bertie," said Marmaduke; he didn't actually say 'that bounder Bertie,' but it was in his tone and made Freddie wonder if there was something between the two that he ought to know about.

"Well, that was a long time ago and she's married to Marcus now," said Dotty.

"Only last summer. I never understood how she wound up married to that awful old stick," Marmaduke responded sulkily. "It's hardly better than marrying Bertie."

"It's a mystery to us all, Marmalade," Bicky said sympathetically. "I don't see what business she had getting married to anybody at her age. These aren't the dear old days, dead beyond recall, when a girl got shoved off onto the first chap her family could catch for her and never asked her how she liked it." He sounded nearly as resentful about his younger sister's marriage as Marmaduke did. "If you'd asked me, they might've done much better for her, old thing."

Marmaduke diffidently kicked the trunk of a tree in reply.

"I was afraid Uncle Kell would make a scene when it came his turn to speak," said Dotty. "What if he'd accused Kell right there over his son's body? Could the family ever recover from that? As if we haven't provided enough scandal already to keep our neighbors busy gossiping for months. By the way, Freddie, what's this about Kell intending to leave old Blighty?"

The question jolted Freddie from pondering Bicky's and Marmaduke's intriguing conversation. "How did you learn about that?" he wondered.

"I overheard Uncle Win telling Aunt Emily. Is it true?" All the cousins looked extremely interested in Freddie's answer.

"I don't know if he truly means it, but it's what he told me when I saw him this morning," he said. "I had to tell Uncle Winthrop, in hopes it would make him change his mind."

"I hope it does too, but it won't get Kell out of the trouble he's in," said Dotty. "That policeman won't beg off now just because Uncle Win tells him to. It'd only make him more suspicious of Kell than he already is."

"I wish there was something we could do for Kell," said Bicky, "but short of confessing to murder ourselves, what can we do? I'm not quite ready to go that far."

"If he's arrested, we could help Phil to break him free from prison," replied his brother, "only they haven't actually arrested him and I sincerely hope they never do."

"It's good of you lads to stand by Kell," said Freddie. "He needs his friends, especially now."

"Why shouldn't we stick by him?" Dotty responded. "Because of Phil? What business is that of ours? Kell's our cousin as much as yours. Besides, however much Uncle Win fusses about it, Kell and Phil haven't done anything we haven't all done too." He grinned. "I expect every one of us got up to precisely the same sort of games at school. I daresay Chubbs here could tell us a thing or two about you, Freddie. You shared a room for three years."

"Afraid not, old chap," said Chubbs. "Not with Freddie anyway. He doesn't go in for it."

"Don't you?" Dotty regarded his cousin skeptically. "Not even with Kell?"

"No," said Freddie, though he didn't expect to be believed. Kell was, after all, his closest friend.

"Well, most of us did," said Bicky. "We grew out of it once we were out of school and caught sight of a girl or two." They had come to the end of the woodland path and arrived at the edge of the front lawn of the Hall near the drive where cars returning from the funeral were unloading their passengers. Celia was helping her husband out of one car; Beatrice and Louisa had just emerged from another. Bicky and Marmaduke exchanged another sympathetic glance. "Kell hasn't, that's all."

"If Uncle Win was honest, he'd remember that things probably weren't very different in his school days," his brother said, and both of them and Eustace chuckled.

The boys quickly stifled their laughter, for Louisa had left her aunt and was headed in their direction.

"If you ask me," said Bicky, "Uncle Win wouldn't even care so much about Kell's behavior if he wasn't so eager to see him married. He isn't as keen to see us marry." He smiled at Louisa as she drew near, and she shyly smiled in return.

"It might be better if Kell did go away for awhile," Chubbs said quietly to Freddie, so that his sister wouldn't overhear. "Not out of England, of course, but away from Marsh Hall once this unpleasantness is over and done with. It'd do him a world of good to get away from these Marshes. That is–" He paused, flustered. "I beg your pardon. I didn't mean–"

"Quite all right, Chubbs." Dotty smiled. "We know we aren't the Marshes you're referring to, and anyway, I agree with you."

"But Kell can't go away," said Louisa, who had overheard after all. "It wouldn't be fair, not if he's innocent as we all know he is." She looked appealingly from one young man to another. "You do believe he's innocent, don't you?"

"Of course we do," Bicky answered. "Nobody in their right mind could think otherwise." He received another shy smile.

"It's ridiculous!" Dotty agreed. "Why, I've got as much reason to get rid of Bertie as Kell did. With both him and Bertie out of the way, I'd be next in line as heir. Or it might've been Bicky."

"Me?" cried his brother. "What reason would I have?"

"Once the way was clear, you'd only have to give me a good knock over the head to get rid of me too."

"Louisa, dear," Beatrice called her away from the group of boys.

"It's a pity Kell doesn't take an interest in girls," said Chubbs as Louisa returned to their aunt. "Lou's grown up rather nice, if I do say so as a brother. And she's so obviously sweet on him."

"Obviously," echoed Bicky, and Chubbs looked contrite again.

As the others headed into Marsh Hall by the front door, Freddie went around to the side of the house to walk across the garden lawn toward the boathouse. Before he had crossed the terrace, however, he spotted a figure standing beneath the row of willows at the edge of the river, half-hidden by the curtain of long leaves, waving to draw his attention. It was Billy.

"I've just come from the boathouse," Billy announced once Freddie had crossed the garden lawn and ducked under the fringe of willow leaves to join him.

"What did you find out?"

In response, Billy took a small notebook out of the pocket of his jacket; Freddie smiled at the sight of it, for it reminded him of Constable Hobart, and Billy explained, "You said we ought to be methodical, so I thought as I'd better write it all down to be sure I got it right. Now then," he opened the tiny book and read from his notes, "Mr. Bertram Marsh went to the boathouse straight after breakfast. The boatsmen say he was alone when he rowed off, and that was the last they saw of him. He didn't tell them where he was going. They said they told the police just the same the day after Mr. Bertram went missing, and didn't have more to add."

"What about Dotty?" asked Freddie. "Did he take a boat too?"

"Mr. Daed'lus Marsh took a boat out less 'n an hour after Mr. Bertie, but here's an odd thing: He didn't bring it back. His brother, Mr. Icarus, did."

"Bicky? Are they quite sure of that?"

"Well, they allow it's easy enough to get the two brothers mixed up, as they look so much alike, but one of the old boatsmen, Mr. Tubworth, his name is, swears it was Icarus Marsh that came back to the boathouse just before noon."

"Yes, I remember Old Tubby," said Freddie. "He's been with the family for years. He'd know one lad from the other. Bicky said he slept late that morning, but he must've been lying. Did you look into that?"

"I did, and that makes what the boatsmen told me odder still." Billy turned back to the first page in his notebook. "I asked the housemaid that does the family's rooms. We had a nice chat while you were sleeping. She says Mr. Icarus was snoring very loud when she went to straighten his room. She didn't try to go in then, but came back just before lunch. Early that morning, she was taking water up to your cousins' rooms as she does for 'em most days, but she says he was quiet then. She knocked on the door, but there wasn't no answer."

"He must've been out earlier and come back to the house," Freddie mused. "But why would he do that? It doesn't make sense. Why go out, then come back in for a nap, and then go out again at noon to return Dotty's boat? What could he and Dotty have been up to?" As they walked away from the house, he turned briefly to glance back. "What about the others, Chubbs and Mellie?"

"Miss Amelia was out all day, and didn't come back 'til dinner-time with her sister, Miss Agatha," Billy reported.

"Yes, that fits with what Mellie told me. She walked over to visit Agatha at her studio."

"And as far as anyone can say, Mr. Charles Burke didn't come to the Hall 'til two days ago."

"Oxford's about 120 miles away. I suppose it's possible that a fast car like Kell's little roadster can manage that in about 3 hours by way of the back roads past Milton Keyes and Bedford. I don't know if Chubbs has such a car at his disposal, but he might've borrowed one from a friend. He could've driven here unseen, then gone home again, but I can't think of a reason why he would." Freddie laughed. "I find it rather difficult to imagine old Chubbs driving fast as a demon across the home counties with murder on his mind, don't you?"

"It does make an odd picture," Billy agreed, "but there's one other person you didn't ask about that might've brought him down from Oxford in a hurry: Miss Louisa Burke was missing for an hour or more that morning."

"Louisa?"

"She turned up again at lunch, right as rain, but Effie said that her aunt, Miss Beatrice Burke, was making the biggest fuss, setting the whole house upside down looking for her."

"Yes, Aunt Beatrice watches over Louisa very closely. Would she have sent for Chubbs if his sister went missing?" Freddie shook his head. "What a peculiar business this is! Bicky, Dotty, possibly Chubbs, and now Louisa—was anyone where they said they were?"

He and Billy had been walking slowly up the footpath beneath the willows in the direction of the cottage lane. As they emerged from the cover of the last willow, Freddie stopped suddenly. He could see that someone was crouched on the riverbank; Inspector Deffords was examining the spot where the boat had been.

17

Freddie waved for Billy to stay where he was and went on ahead. As he drew closer, he could see that Deffords was examining the footprints in the mud. The inspector turned his head slightly at the sound of someone approaching on the embankment above him but didn't look up. Freddie felt that he had to speak first.

"I saw you at the funeral. I thought that you were meant to keep watch over my cousin Kell."

"I gave Constable Hobart that duty," Deffords replied, then looked up at Freddie. "I thought it was more important to see the Marsh family and their guests today. You suggested this morning that I ought to pay more attention to them."

"Was there anyone you paid particular attention to?" Freddie asked.

"You, for one. The other pallbearers, especially the boys I hadn't seen before. His Lordship and his brother. The young lady who was crying at the end."

"My cousin Agatha."

"I questioned her the other day at her studio. Hobart tells me that she's one of the 'American'

Marshes. She doesn't sound like an American."

"She isn't, really," Freddie explained. "That's what the local folk call her and her brother and sister. Their father came from the United States, but they were born here at the Hall just as the rest of us were. I don't think they've visited their American relatives more than once or twice, and that was before the war when Uncle Martin was alive."

"I didn't realize she was so close to the dead boy."

"I didn't either until this morning," Freddie confided. "Their engagement hadn't been announced yet, but I gather that there was some sort of understanding."

"Your people always marry their cousins."

Freddie laughed. "Oh, they're not so close in that respect! The 'American' Marshes are something like 5th or 6th cousins to us, hardly related by blood at all, though of course we always think of them as our family." He was at ease as he explained to Deffords how Charles Burke and Marmaduke and Eustace Marsh were related to the family at the Hall. Then, feeling emboldened, he ventured, "May I ask what brought you here, Inspector, if it isn't prying into police business? You must've come directly from the church."

Deffords didn't mind answering this question. "You also suggested that I have another look at this place. Photographs were taken by my sergeant when we first arrived. I can see that someone's been here since then. There are two new sets of footprints. Someone went wading." He pointed to indicate the traces of Freddie's bare feet heading into the rushes.

"Yes, that was me," Freddie admitted. "I thought I saw something in the water."

"What did you find?"

"Nothing important." Since talking to Kell, Freddie was more certain than ever that the broken piece of jewelry was a vital clue, but he was determined to say nothing about it until he learned who it belonged to. If the woman was someone Kell cared enough to protect, then she must be someone that he cared for as well. He wouldn't betray her without hearing her side of the story.

"There's another set of bare footprints," said Deffords. "Not yours. A woman's."

"Then you did notice them?"

"It's my job to notice. Yes, we made note of them when I first examined the scene. Is that what you wanted me to see?"

"As a matter of fact, it was. I had an idea that a girl was in the boat with Bertie. Bill—my manservant—" Freddie gestured toward his friend, who stood some distance down the footpath, "says that he's heard gossip among the Hall servants that my cousin was a nuisance to the maids." That was true, at least, and would direct the inspector's attention away from the ladies in the household. "I don't suppose you consider that very seriously, or you'd be looking about for girls already."

"There isn't enough left to identify her, only part of a heel and some toes. Not enough to make a cast. And she might've been here long before your cousin was killed. The other prints, even Bertram Marsh's, cover hers. All the same, I'll have a word with your Bill." Deffords had risen from his crouched position and was regarding

Billy, though not with the same degree of mistrust and suspicion which Billy regarded him. "He doesn't act like a servant. You don't speak to him like one."

Deffords could only have heard him speaking to Billy at the George and Dragon just before they'd met. He had overheard their conversation. "We're friends as well," said Freddie. "He saved my life twice during the war. His father is employed by Uncle Hill, and I've known him since we were children. Kell and I used to spend our school holidays there."

"All boys together," Deffords said dryly. "Do you know, Mr. Babington, the most frustrating part of investigating a murder among a close group of people? No one will tell you anything. They're all concerned with protecting each other. That's natural, but it doesn't make my work any easier." He met Freddie's eyes suddenly and said, "Do you think I haven't guessed what the quarrel between Captain Marsh and his father was about?"

Freddie was once again startled at how the inspector went straight back to this point. "A guess isn't the same as proof," he answered, feeling as if he were on dangerous ground. "Are– are you really so determined to suspect Kell until you know the truth about that?"

"It isn't a policeman's job to suspect anyone, Mr. Babington. I'm here to gather information and evidence and see where it leads me. When I have enough evidence to prove that one person committed this murder, I'll make my arrest. That's how real detectives solve crimes. I have a question that no one seems willing to answer. That makes it important, at least until I know the answer. I think you can tell me, and I think you will if it'll help your cousin. You want to help your cousin, don't you?"

"Yes," said Freddie. "I want nothing more desperately than to keep Kell from being arrested. But I simply can't tell you what you want to know."

"What if I tell you that I'm considering other people besides Captain Marsh? Nicholas Marsh has nothing good to say of his great-nephew Bertram, and he is rarely out without his golf clubs. Marcus Marsh has a pretty young wife who used to run around with his cousin, and he carries a heavy cane with a brass handle. His wife also has two brothers—one admits to being out on the river that morning. Would you rather I suspect one of them instead of Captain Marsh?"

In light of the curious things Billy had told him about Dotty and Bicky, this last remark struck home. "I'd rather it not be any of my family," he answered, "but under the circumstances, I don't see how it can be avoided."

18

When Freddie left Deffords, he was pale and shaken by their conversation. Billy, who stood waiting for him atop the embankment, reached down to take his arm and help him up.

"What'd that man say to upset you?" he hissed as Freddie scrambled onto the footpath. He threw a hostile look at the inspector, who was watching them from about a hundred yards away.

"He's dangerous, Billy," Freddie told his friend in an undertone. "He knows that I know about Kell and he's determined to have the truth from me.

I'm afraid if he keeps at me, he might get it."

"He won't out of me!" Billy declared defiantly.

"Good lad! He wants to talk to you about gossip in the servants' hall. Tell him whatever you like about Bertie, but not about the jewelry I found."

Billy nodded, and went down to be questioned.

Freddie left them. He still felt unsettled as he crossed the garden lawn and went inside Marsh Hall by way of the garden door to the parlor where Bertie's coffin had been. As he walked down the empty hallway, he first went past the library, where Uncle Stephen and Dr. Grant were having an abstruse argument about the comparative attributes of saints and demigods; it might have interested Freddie under other circumstances, but the voices of his other uncles from within Lord Marshbourne's study captured his attention:

"-'til you know the truth of the matter, it's only just," Kellynch was saying, his voice rising with emotion. "That's all I ask for, Win—justice for my son."

"What about my son? It's hard on the boy if he's innocent, harder than I thought it'd be if he's talking of leaving England rather than give in."

"If he's innocent, then there'll be proof of it. And if you're afraid of Kell's running off, then keeping him under watch is the best way to see he stays right where he is."

Winthrop sighed. "Yes, I suppose you're right."

Freddie's heart sank at this exchange. He stole quietly past the study door and down the hallway to the drawing room, where the rest of the family and their guests had gathered to partake of refreshments after the funeral. The drawing room was large, well-proportioned, and well-furnished, full of comfortable chairs and settees, but very crowded that day. Emily was pouring cups of tea, and footmen served cake, scones, and finger sandwiches. Since Freddie was late coming in, there were no empty seats; once he'd been given his tea, he found a place to stand near the mantelpiece, beneath a large portrait of his aunt. From this vantage point, he could keep an eye on Dotty and Bicky, who were at the other end of the room, wedged in behind the chair their mother was sitting in. He meant to speak to them once he could catch them alone.

Theresa and her daughters were absent, but their absence made them a prime topic of conversation. Some disapproving murmurs about Agatha's behavior were heard among the guests. Tears were naturally expected at a funeral, but so public an exhibition of deep, personal grief was a shocking display in bad taste.

"Questionable taste it may have been, but I can't blame the poor child. I feel quite sorry for her," Matilda declared. "It's a terrible thing to happen to a girl. To lose your fiancé!" She shook her head sadly. "Poor Agatha won't even have memories of happier times, and it will be so much harder for her to give her heart to someone else after this tragedy."

Other ladies in the room were likewise sympathetic, but some disagreed about the correctness of Agatha's conduct, broken heart or no broken heart. The question might've become an argument, if it hadn't ended abruptly when Amelia came in.

"How is your sister, dear?" Emily asked her.

"She's calmer now, Aunt Emily. We've put her to bed and Mother's sitting by her." Amelia accepted the cup of tea her aunt offered. Her brother, who was seated nearby, gave her his place and leant on his cane. "I've never seen her so upset before. It's hardly like her. But I don't believe in this stiff-upper lip nonsense. If Agatha feels like weeping over Bertie, why shouldn't she? Hardly anyone has." Amelia showed no signs of mourning herself, only a defiant protectiveness for her sister, as if she knew very well what the older ladies had been saying. "Agatha wants to go back to her cottage as soon she's fit, and I'm going with her to look after her. She can have peace and quiet there, and it'll do her good to be among her own things."

"It might do her good to return to her work," said Emily. "It will help to take her mind off her sorrows."

"Yes, I think so too," Mellie agreed. "So does Mother."

"A girl as artistic as Agatha must of course be very sensitive," Sarah Marsh observed. "Is she still painting her pictures?" Agatha's paintings were a noteworthy peculiarity, since they were more than ladylike watercolor daubs. She had actually sold her work in London galleries, and newspaper articles had spoken of her striking style.

"Yes, she is. She's really rather talented, you know," Marcus informed them. "She mostly paints pictures of gardens, flowers, ivy-covered cottages and such-like, but she does portraits too."

"She did a lovely picture of Marcus and

Cecelia to commemorate their wedding," Matilda added proudly. "And she painted that." She indicated the portrait of Emily. "It's very beautiful work, isn't it? An excellent likeness." The style wasn't so modern that the subject was unrecognizable and showed a pre-Raphaelite influence in the vibrant color of Emily's strawberry hair and the expression in her eyes. Those visitors who hadn't been in the drawing room to see this portrait before expressed their appreciation of it.

"Agatha promised me one of Winthrop, to match," said Emily. "Perhaps she'll paint it, once she's sufficiently recovered from her loss."

Freddie sipped his tea and continued to watch Dotty and Bicky. He paid little attention to what was being said, for his thoughts were scattered in other directions.

What had his two cousins been up to on the river that day? Was Louisa Burke part of it, or was her disappearance due to some other matter entirely? For an instant, Freddie considered the possibility that she might be the girl seen in Bertie's boat, then he dismissed the idea. Louisa could never be described as 'dark-haired,' and she was too innocent a young girl for such goings-on with the likes of Bertie... wasn't she?

He couldn't help thinking of that ridiculous joke Dotty had made on their walk back from the funeral. He would've thought it nothing more than Dotty's usual nonsense, if Kell hadn't said nearly the same thing. Freddie had first considered Dotty's mysterious actions in connection with Celia, but he doubted now that Celia was involved in this at all. Did Dotty have more selfish reasons for wanting rid of Bertie? Now that Bertie was dead, what if Kell were hanged for his murder or fled the country forever? Daedelus Marsh would become the next Lord Marshbourne. Was that reason enough to kill one cousin and keep silent while another was accused of the crime? Would his brother assist him?

No, it was too ridiculous. Freddie couldn't believe it, not of Dotty and Bicky.

At last, Dotty made his excuses and squeezed out from behind his mother's chair. Bicky slipped out after him. They left the drawing room. Freddie left his teacup on the mantelpiece and followed.

He caught up with the pair at the foot of the stair going up to their bedrooms and took the elder boy by the arm. "Dotty, wait a moment. I want to talk to you—to both of you." Bicky stopped a few steps higher up. "I'd like to ask you some questions about what you said at dinner last night. Dotty, didn't you tell everyone that you went fishing at Upper Lock pool the morning Bertie was killed?"

Both boys looked curious at the question. Dotty nodded. "Yes, that's right."

"Phil says you were at Thicket Cottage. Which is it?"

"Thicket Cottage," his cousin answered after a hesitation. "Once I learned what Kell's quarrel with his father was about, I wanted to give my support to him and Phil, so I went to see them. Kell wasn't in, but Phil and I had a talk instead. Why do you ask?"

"Because you were out on the river when Bertie was killed," Freddie pursued. "If you went to see Kell and Phillip, you must've gone downstream just as Bertie did and landed your boat at the same place on the bank. Were you there when he was?

Did you see him? I want the truth."

Dotty laughed at first, then stared at him in astonishment. "Freddie Babington, what are you thinking? Are you actually asking if I had something to do with Bertie's death?"

"No." Freddie blushed in spite of himself. Hadn't he been thinking just that? "But you lied about your whereabouts and I want to know why. It was such a silly lie. Honestly, Dotty, you should have at least asked Phil to keep his mouth shut."

"I wasn't trying to hide the truth from you, Freddie. It was Uncle Win I didn't want to know. There's no chance that he'd talk to Phil with things as they are now."

"Then why did you bring it up at the table last night, when you might've easily said nothing?"

"Well, I am on Kell's side, you know, and I thought I had to say something on his behalf. Where I really was didn't alter my point about Kell's being suspected for such flimsy reasons. Besides," Dotty lowered his voice, "last night, I said my position was no better than Kell's. You can see now that, except for that quarrel with his father, it's nearly the same. If the police thought I had a reason to want rid of Bertie, I could be in Kell's place."

"Your position is worse than that," Freddie told him. "What were you and Bicky up to when you played that trick with the boat?"

The question took both brothers completely by surprise. "You know about that too?" asked Bicky.

"I asked the boatmen," said Freddie. "You're lucky that no one else has. If the police weren't so interested in Kell, the two of you might be in serious trouble." He looked from one boy to the other. "What were you doing? Please, tell me."

Dotty glanced at his brother; Bicky nodded, giving him permission to speak. "If you must know, Bicky wanted to get away for awhile and not have anyone know about it. He's awfully sweet on her."

"Who?" Freddie asked. Then, in a flash of comprehension, he understood. "Louisa Burke?"

"It's a secret," said Bicky. "Uncle Win and Louisa's Aunt Beatrice wouldn't approve it. They'd rather see her marry Kell."

"Is that why she was asked here?" asked Freddie.

"You didn't see how Uncle Win was pushing the poor girl at Kell. Kell tried to be kind to her, but he wasn't going to let himself be married off no matter who his father picked out for him. You know how badly that turned out."

"It's not that Kell objected to Louisa in particular," Dotty added. "It's just that after all the others, she was the final straw."

Freddie remembered what Kell had told him about 'half a dozen girls' being paraded before him as prospective brides. "There were a lot of others, weren't there?"

"Just about any suitable girl," said Dotty. "Right after Kell came home, Uncle Win started off by talking to him about Mellie, then Aunt Delphinia's Barlow nieces and your cousin Angela. He's got a grudge against the Tollarhithes right now because of Phil, but last winter he thought that Kell might agree to marry one of Phil's sisters—as if it'd be the next best thing! But Kell didn't like that idea either. Then Uncle Win invited Louisa to come for the Easter vac."

"I've spent a lot of time with Louisa since she came here," Bicky continued. "She's a very sweet girl. I wanted to protect her."

"From Bertie," Dotty explained. "He was always around Louisa too, but that was mainly because he knew she was meant for Kell and he could never resist trying his charms on a pretty girl."

"Aunt Beatrice didn't mind him, though," said Bicky. "Since Bertie was courting Agatha, she didn't see any harm in it. But once she saw that I was buzzing 'round her precious chick, she started whisking Louisa off whenever I tried to talk to her. You've seen how Aunt Beatrice watches over her. There's no chance to speak to the girl alone. I hoped that if I could get Louisa away from her awful aunt for awhile, I might be able to tell her that if Kell didn't care for her, I did. If it turned out that she liked me too, we could wait 'til this trouble with Kell was past and once Uncle Winthrop got over his disappointment, he mightn't mind having a nephew married to a nice girl with a modest fortune instead of his son."

"What did you do, exactly?" Freddie asked. "Where did you go?"

The brothers exchanged a quizzical look. Dotty answered first. "I didn't go up the river, Freddie. I never saw Bertie after breakfast that morning. After I got the boat, I took it downstream a few hundred yards from the boathouse and hid it in the willows that hang over the river, where Bicky and I had planned. I waited 'til Bicky came down to the spot with Louisa, and they got into the boat. Once I saw them off, I went back to the Hall, and climbed up the oak tree to get in Bicky's bedroom window."

"I'd gone out the same way," Bicky added, "and left it unlatched for Dotty to get in."

"I was going to pretend to be Bicky, in case anyone went looking for him once Aunt Beatrice noticed Louisa was missing," Dotty explained. "There was an awful fuss when she did, but whenever I heard someone coming, I snored as loudly as I could 'til they went away."

"Dotty, that sounds like a ridiculous plan," Freddie observed.

"Well, it worked, didn't it? Bicky and Louisa got off for a couple of hours by themselves, and no one knows where they were."

"Then you went to Thicket Cottage?"

Dotty nodded. "When things quieted down and I thought I'd been there long enough so that everyone would believe Bicky was in his room sleeping and hadn't gone running off with Louisa, I went out the window again. I walked over to Marshbanks by way of the wood and stopped to visit Kell and Phil. I was never near the river once I came back to the Hall. Does that satisfy your curiosity, Freddie?"

"Yes, thank you. What about you, Bicky?" Freddie turned to his other cousin. "Where did you go?"

"Surely you don't think I had anything to do with Bertie's death?" Bicky protested. "Not with Louisa in the boat with me. Or do you think she's in on it too?"

"I think he's gone quite mad," said Dotty. "Suspecting us?" He didn't sound as indignant as his brother, but puzzled by this questioning and somewhat concerned.

"I haven't gone mad," Freddie tried to

assure them. "I only want to help Kell by finding out what really happened that day. I'm sorry if I sound suspicious, but you must admit that your comings-and-goings looked a little strange. It was a mystery that had to be cleared up."

Thus appealed to, Bicky was placated enough to answer, "Well, if you must know, Louisa and I let the current carry us downstream past the village, then we had to row back furiously to be home in time for lunch. I left her off under the willow trees before I took the boat back."

"Does Chubbs know about this adventure of yours?"

"Yes, of course," said Bicky. "We told him when he arrived and heard how Louisa had gone missing. I wanted him to know there was no cause for alarm, that she was perfectly safe the whole time."

"Did you tell him that Bertie was paying attentions to Louisa?" Freddie still found it difficult to imagine sturdy, even-tempered Chubbs in a murderous rage, but if Bertie had trifled with his young sister, that might be just the thing to do it.

"No," said Dotty. "Why should we? Bertie was dead by then. You aren't suspecting Chubbs now, are you?"

"No, I only thought I'd ask." It occurred to Freddie that it was probably Bicky and Louisa, dark-haired or not, who'd been seen rowing on the river—not Bertie and some other girl at all. His best theory was crushed. "How did it turn out?" he asked Bicky. "Do you and Louisa have an understanding now?"

"No, it's just as her brother said: she's sweet

on Kell," Bicky answered sulkily. "Poor Louisa was broken-hearted that he didn't want to marry her. She told me I was very kind to think of her and perhaps someday she might think of me the same way, but she couldn't right now. I left it at that. It didn't seem fair to go on after that. This false accusation against Kell has only made him more attractive to her. Unless Uncle Winthrop changes his mind..."

"He won't," Freddie said. "Uncle Kellynch's talked him out of it. By the way, what did you and Marmaduke mean when you were talking about Celia and her choice of husband?"

"Marmalade's in love with her, that's all. He was here last summer when she came out of school and he noticed that she wasn't a little girl anymore. They played tennis, croquet, went out rowing, that sort of thing. Well, he's only just 22 and still at university, so he didn't feel he could speak up, but he thought there'd be plenty of time. Who could imagine she'd marry Marcus? I certainly didn't."

"I still don't believe it," added Dotty.

"If it'd been our choice, we'd much rather have Marm for a brother-in-law than Marcus or Bertie. Here, Freddie, I hope you don't think Marmalade had anything to do with this murder. He was miles away when it happened."

"What good would it do him to kill Bertie? If it was Marcus who'd gone into the river, then you might have some reason to suspect him."

Freddie had to agree. Though it seemed improbable, he thought he ought to ask one last question before he finished with his cousins. "I don't suppose either of you know if Louisa had a pin or earrings made up of silver leaves with garnets?"

Was it his imagination, or was there a look of complicity between the two brothers?

"I don't think so," said Bicky. "Not Louisa."

"No," Dotty spoke more decisively. "Certainly not."

19

Billy followed Freddie's instructions and told Inspector Deffords about the girl who'd been seen in the boat, but not about the girl Nicholas Marsh had seen in the lane. He didn't mention the piece of jewelry Freddie had found, but repeated most of his conversation with Effie regarding the antics of Bertram Marsh. He was ready to keep his mouth firmly shut on the subject of Kell's quarrel with his father, and was somewhat disappointed when the inspector didn't even ask.

When he returned to the Hall, he sought out Effie to see if she could tell him more about the maid whose husband who had wanted to fight Bertie. These two were the only people he'd heard of who might want Bertram dead and were not part of the Marsh family. Finding them might draw Deffords' attention away from the Marshes. Freddie would also want him to talk to them if possible. Effie might be able to tell him where Milly's family lived, or where the husband's farm was. He asked in the kitchens and one of the undercooks directed him out to the wash yard beyond the kitchen garden.

It was a household laundry day. Washing was done in the old-fashioned way in numerous huge boiling coppers and wooden washtubs in the laundry house, which was some distance from the Hall and screened from it by a tall hedge. The last of the washing was done by the time Billy arrived; gallons of soapy water had been dumped out onto the drainage tiles. The laundry house had drying rooms, but since it was a sunny spring day, the wash had been strung up on lines across the wash yard.

Billy scanned the group of maids taking down the first dried sheets and clothing, searching for that head of bright yellow hair, when he noticed something that he hadn't been looking for. His mouth dropped open.

After he'd left Dotty and Bicky, Freddie went to his room to lie down. His head was buzzing as he tried to puzzle matters out. While he'd found answers to several of his most perplexing questions, he didn't feel as if he were any closer to solving the central problem of who had killed Bertie. And was any of it of help to Kell?

He was jolted from his thoughts when the door to his room opened. "Freddie!" Billy burst in eagerly. "There's something you got to see, if she's still there."

"'She'?"

"Come on." Taking Freddie by the arm, Billy hauled him from the bed, out into the hallway and down the servants' stairs. At the bottom, they went out through a door by the scullery, through the kitchen garden and into the wash yard.

"I came here looking for Effie," Billy said breathlessly. "I didn't find her, but I saw this other girl–" He nodded to indicate one of the maids who stood chatting and laughing among a group around a large wicker basket. "Freddie, look. *Her*, there."

Freddie looked, but he didn't see what was so interesting about the maid at first, until she turned toward them. Then he saw it: at the hollow of her throat was a pendant made up of silver loops like tiny leaves and sparkling garnets.

"It's just like that bit you found," Billy hissed near his ear.

"Who is she?" Freddie whispered back. "Do you know her?"

"I've seen her in the servants' hall. Lily's her name. She's maid to some of the ladies. D'you think she's the one?"

"It could be." Freddie felt his hopes rising. So the mysterious dark-haired girl might exist after all! "That necklace is too expensive to belong to a maidservant. If she's the one we've been looking for, Bertie must've given it to her as a gift." In spite of himself, his imagination took flight again. "If he was dallying with this girl, they might've been going to one of the cottages for a tryst."

"I thought you said that bit of jewelry belonged to one of the family?" asked Billy. "Why else would Cap'n Kell not tell us about it?"

"Yes, that's what I thought," Freddie admitted. "But I must've been mistaken. There must be some other reason for Kell to keep silent. We've got to find out. Go and talk to her, Billy."

Billy balked. "What do I say?"

"Flirt with her."

"Flirt?"

"Oh, you know the sort of thing. Tell her she's pretty. She's got lovely eyes. Say something about how the garnets in that pendant bring out the red in her hair, and then ask where she got it. Lead up to the question gradually." Billy was staring at him incredulously. "I've got to know," Freddie explained. "I can't ask her, Bill—it wouldn't be right for one of the family to be so familiar with a maid. Or, worse, she might think I'm accusing her of stealing it. She'll be much more likely to tell you the truth if you ask her in the right way."

Billy nodded, agreeing reluctantly.

"All right then." Freddie gave him a push to send him off. "Go on!"

While Billy approached the maid, Freddie retreated to a bench in one corner of the yard, where he could watch his friend's progress without being too conspicuous; the servants who noticed him seemed curious at the sight of a gentleman in a black frock coat hanging about their work area. A good thing he'd left his top hat in his room. He wished he'd brought his cigarette case with him, however, for it would at least give him the visible excuse of sitting out here for a quiet smoke.

The maid Lily had stripped down one line of clothing and was dragging her laundry basket toward the next. Billy caught up with her and, taking the handle at one end of the basket, offered to carry it for her. The two began to chat as he helped her take down a line of bed-sheets. Lily didn't seem to find the attention unwelcome, but smiled, laughed, and touched her hair, until Freddie began to believe that Billy was enjoying his task after all. He also noticed that some of the other maids nearby looked jealous that the visitor had picked out Lily to talk to.

Freddie had to admit that once Billy

overcame his natural shyness, he had a way with women. He was comfortable talking to them. It was an ability that Freddie acknowledged he didn't possess himself. He felt awkward around girls he hadn't known from childhood. Never mind that it wasn't proper—he simply couldn't have brought himself to flirt with a girl as he'd instructed Billy to do.

When Lily had filled her laundry basket, Billy carried it for her to the yard entrance, where two other maids were waiting to bring their baskets in. Billy said something to make them laugh. An older woman in charge of the laundry ordered them to get on about their business and, with one last smile at him, Lily followed the other girls in the direction of the Hall. Once they had gone, Billy looked around, found Freddie, and went to him. He was rather flushed in the face.

"Well?" asked Freddie.

"It wasn't Mr. Bertram," Billy reported. "Lily told me it was one of the ladies she tends. She said, 'Miss Amelia gave it me.'"

20

Freddie retrieved the broken piece of jewelry from the pocket of the coat he'd worn that morning and returned to the drawing room. The last of the visitors were departing and the tea things had been cleared away. The family was dispersing to their rooms to change out of their funeral clothes before dinner. Amelia had already gone. He hoped to see her at the dinner table, but Amelia stayed to watch over her sister and let Theresa, who had been sitting by Agatha's bedside all afternoon, come down to dinner instead.

Since Amelia's room wasn't far down the hall from Freddie's own, he decided that his best chance to catch her was by keeping his bedroom door ajar and waiting until she went to bed. After dinner, he pulled a chair close behind the door and settled down for his vigil with the fragment of jewelry between his fingers. Billy sat to wait with him, perched on the foot of the bed.

"D'you think Miss Amelia's the girl who was seen in Mr. Bertram's boat?" Billy wondered.

"I don't know." Even when Freddie had guessed that Amelia was the one Uncle Nicholas had seen, he'd never thought that she also must be the mysterious dark-haired girl seen with Bertie. And yet Bertie seemed to have pursued every other girl-cousin at the Hall: Celia, Agatha, even Louisa. Why not Mellie too? "It seems incredible, but how else could she have lost this by the river if she hadn't been there herself?"

"It looks as if you were right in the first place," said Billy. "Cap'n Kell must've known it was hers."

"Yes, and I think Celia recognized it when I showed it to her. Dotty and Bicky did too." Freddie recalled the glance that had gone between the two brothers when he'd described the fragment of jewelry to them.

"Why'd he lie about it? Cap'n Kell's not sweet on this cousin of yours, is he? The way he's stuck by Mr. Phillip, I'd've thought he didn't care for any girl."

"It isn't like that," Freddie explained. "Mellie's like a sister to him. You have to understand how we were brought up together. You haven't been up to the nursery, have you? It's shut now, 'til there are children in the household again. It fills the entire top floor of the Hall, bedrooms and playrooms and cubbies for nursery-maids. We grew up there, the whole lot of us, tumbled atop each other like puppies in a basket. I didn't have a room of my own until I was ten, after I came home from school for the first time. You grow very close under those conditions. We are a close family, perhaps too close." He played with the broken fragment, then turned to Billy. "Wouldn't you do the same if it were one of your sisters, Bill? You'd lie to protect Mabel or Margie?"

"Probably," Billy admitted, "but I'd hope they'd speak up before I'd got myself hung for something I didn't do." Then, after a delicate pause, he asked, "D'you think she killed him?"

"Mellie? No." Freddie shook his head briskly. "No, I can't believe that. Mellie's a dear. She wouldn't ever deliberately harm anyone."

Billy huffed at this. "Well, it seems to me–" he began, when another door down the hallway creaked open.

"Hush!" Freddie hissed. He left his seat and crept toward the door to peek out; Amelia was just emerging from Agatha's room. Freddie went out to intercept her.

Amelia jumped and looked startled. "Freddie? What? Is something the matter?"

"I've been waiting to talk to you, Mellie. It's important. I believe I've found something that belongs to you." He held up the broken piece of jewelry.

If he'd had any doubts, they disappeared as he watched the color drain from Amelia's face.

"Wh– where did you find that?"

"In the shallows of the river, near where Bertie was drowned," Freddie told her. "It is yours, isn't it?"

Amelia stared at him wildly, then said, "Not here, come inside." Grabbing Freddie by the arm, she yanked him abruptly into her room. "Shut the door." While Freddie closed the door, his cousin opened the jewelry box on her dressing table and brought out an earring that matched the broken piece.

"It's mine," she confirmed.

"And the necklace?"

"There was a pendant," she answered. "After I lost that one earring, I gave it away."

"Do you know how the earring came to be lost?"

There was another long silence, another moment of decision. When she spoke, her voice was so low that Freddie could barely hear her. "I suppose that Bertie pulled it from my ear when I was struggling with him."

"You were with him that day, on the boat?"

She nodded.

Freddie asked the next question as gently as he could. "Mellie, what happened?"

"You already know all about it," she responded.

"No, not everything. Will you tell me?"

Amelia nodded again. She composed herself, sitting down on her bed and folding her hands in her lap before she began. "I was going to see Agatha. I was walking on the path along the river, when Bertie came rowing by and asked if I'd like to ride with him as he was headed the same way. It would shorten my walk, so I got into the boat." Her hands in her lap clenched more tightly together.

"You took off your shoes."

"That's right. I had stopped at the pool under the willows to dabble my toes in the water. Remember, just the way we did when we were children? It was too cold for it, but I wanted to do it and I didn't think anyone would see. I put my stockings in my coat pocket and carried my shoes. That was when Bertie came along. When we were out in the midst of the water, he proposed to me. At least, that's what I thought it was at first."

"I thought that he and Agatha had an understanding."

The corners of Amelia's mouth turned down. "So did I, but when I said so, Bertie told me, 'That's all over and done with.' He said he was going to break it off with her. She wasn't the one he truly wanted. He went on saying such things, 'til I understood that it wasn't marriage he was proposing. He'd trifled with my sister's heart and he meant to do the same with mine. I wouldn't hear another word of it. Then he tried to kiss me—and I wasn't having any of that from him! I made him row ashore. I said I'd jump out and swim if he didn't. He told me not to be a little fool—I might drown and surely he wasn't as bad as that! So I told him I'd tell Agatha. That did it. But when we got to the bank, he got out of the boat too and grabbed my arm. Perhaps he only meant to stop me from running off to tell tales against him, or perhaps..." She shook her head. "I tried to make him let go. He got hold of my shoulder. I still had my shoes in my hand, so I hit him with them, and hit him again until I was free." The rest of it came out in a breathless burst. "Bertie fell into the water, and I ran away as fast as I could."

Freddie was breathing hard too by the time she finished. "Oh, Mellie. Have you told anyone else about this?"

Amelia opened her mouth, then shut it quickly. After a moment, she said, "No." She looked up at him with large, brown eyes that were tearful and pleading. "Are you going to tell?"

"No," Freddie answered carefully, "but I think you ought to go to the police. They should know the truth of what happened."

"Go to the police?" she repeated, baffled. "What good will that do? Bertie's dead. Why disgrace his name?"

"What about Kell's name?"

"Kell?" She looked more perplexed than before.

"If you'd come forward, Kell would never have fallen under suspicion. The police would've known it was an accident from the first." He sat down beside her and, feeling rather shy even though she was a cousin, took her hand. "You've nothing to be afraid of, Mellie. No one could blame you. You struck Bertie in your own defense. A lady has a right to protect her honor."

Amelia pulled her hand from his with a gasp. "Freddie, I didn't kill Bertie!"

"You didn't?"

"No, of course not! When I last saw Bertie, he'd climbed back to the bank and was sitting by the boat with his head in his hands. His head was bleeding, but he was alive when I left him."

"He was still alive," Freddie murmured,

struggling between relief and doubt.

Amelia regarded him with an odd expression. "You thought I'd killed him, Freddie? That's why you came to talk to me?"

"Yes, I did," he admitted. "When I found your earring by the river, I wondered, I suspected. I'm sorry." He felt ashamed of himself for the second time that day. "But, Mellie, why didn't you say anything before? The truth wouldn't have harmed you, and it would've helped Kell."

"You'll think me a fool, but I didn't consider what happened to me in light of Kell. I was so upset—I didn't want anyone to know. When I heard that Bertie was dead, I didn't think- I mean, I never thought that Kell had killed him, but that someone else must've come along." Her face suddenly went pale and she sat very still, staring straight ahead. She asked in a choked voice, "Did you honestly think I might've done it, by accident? I never meant to strike him so hard, only to make him leave me alone."

"I don't know," Freddie answered. "Perhaps Bertie was dazed and lost his balance and fell into the river. Or maybe he threw himself in because he couldn't bear the shame of what he'd done. Anything of the sort is possible. But it doesn't matter. Don't you see? However Bertie died, it occurred after you'd gone. There's no reason for anyone to believe it wasn't an accident after all."

21

"We've done it, Billy," Freddie announced triumphantly when he returned to his room. "I have my answer!"

Billy still sat at the foot of the bed, where he'd been when Freddie had left. "You know who killed Mr. Bertram?"

"No, not precisely..." Freddie admitted.

"Then what did Miss Amelia tell you?"

"She told me what happened by the river that day, and that was enough." As he prepared for bed, Freddie related the facts of Amelia's story.

"Bertie was sitting by the water's edge when she ran away," he concluded as he buttoned up his pajama top. "I don't know if Bertie fell in after that, or jumped, or was pushed by someone else. The important thing is that we know now how he got the wounds on his head. If Mellie will only speak up, the police will have no other choice but to leave Kell alone."

"You think she's telling the truth?" Billy asked.

Freddie almost laughed with surprise and perhaps a little guilt, since he'd doubted Amelia himself only a short time ago. "What a question! Of course I believe her." A small frown creased his brow. "Why do you think she's lying?"

"I'm not saying she is, nor that she isn't." Billy had been turning a few things over in his own mind while Freddie had been so long in his cousin's bedroom, and he thought he had to speak. "If you don't mind me saying, it seems to me that you're too ready to take these Marshes at their word. What about Mr. Daed'lus? Did you find out what that business of his going out and his brother coming back with the same boat was about?"

"That's turned out to be some silly romantic adventure of Bicky's to court Louisa Burke." Freddie told Billy of his conversation with his cousins. "Dotty and Bicky are silly young asses. It's just the sort of ridiculous stunt they'd put on. I should've guessed it was something of the kind once I heard that Louisa was missing at the same time."

"So you believed them too?"

"Once I heard their story, yes." The small frown deepened. "But, do you know, before we discovered that that earring belonged to Mellie, I was almost certain Dotty was involved in Bertie's death? When I asked him to explain himself, I practically accused him of murder–" Freddie scowled, "because of what you told me."

"I was only doing as you asked!" Billy retorted, stung at this unfairness. "You said we were going to be methodical like a proper detective. Well, if that's what you mean to do then it's no good to go on saying, 'No, Dotty couldn't do this' or 'Mellie wouldn't ever do that,' whenever you find something against them. A real detective like that inspector wouldn't. Now, I know they're your family. You don't like to think they've done wrong, any more'n I'd like to think it of my own brothers or sisters, but you've got to see that if one of 'em did it, they'd lie to you about it."

Billy expected Freddie to explode indignantly at this, but instead, Freddie considered his words seriously.

"You mean that I'm too close to them to be objective?" he asked, and sank down on the bed with a sigh. "You may be right, Billy. I remember my cousins as they were as children, but I haven't lived at the Hall since the year before the war. Nearly ten years. I can't say what they're like now that they're grown, any more than they know who

I am. I've seen what nice people, even respectable, decent Englishmen are capable of. That one of my cousins may have committed murder? I can grasp the idea of it here," he touched the side of his head, "but in my heart, it isn't so simple. I want so much to believe what they say. It feels disloyal to suspect them. These are my nearest relations, almost as dear to me as Kell is. How can I suspect them?" He lifted his eyes to Billy's. "What do you think happened?"

"I couldn't say," Billy admitted. "Maybe Miss Amelia hit Mr. Bertram just like she says, or maybe she hit a bit harder and left him dead. Maybe somebody else came along after she ran off. Maybe it was her brother, or old Mr. Nicholas saw more'n he said and went after Mr. Bertie with one of his golf clubs. Or what about Mr. Daed'lus? He might've gone down the lane after he left Thicket Cottage and come across Mr. Bertie by the river and they had a quarrel. Whatever happened, the one who did it wouldn't tell you—and if any of the others know about it, they wouldn't say either. Seeing how close these Marshes are, they'd stick together. They'd protect each other."

"That inspector said the same thing. But aren't I one of them?"

Billy shook his head. "Not in this. You'll pardon me putting it so, but you've been poking your nose into something they don't want you to know about."

Freddie did laugh at this. "Surely you're not suggesting that they're all in it together? That seems a little far-fetched."

"No, but they aren't telling you everything. They've kept things back, even Cap'n Kell."

"Kell?" Freddie echoed, frown returning.

"You know he wouldn't tell you that that broken bit of earring was Miss Amelia's. Have you thought that Cap'n Kell–" Here, Billy hesitated, afraid he was going too far.

But Freddie wanted to hear it. "What about 'Cap'n Kell,' Billy?" he prompted. A hint of coldness had crept into his voice.

Knowing that he was on dangerous ground, Billy took a deep breath and said, "Have you thought that this story of Miss Amelia's gives him a better reason for getting rid of his cousin than what the police already have against him?"

Freddie gaped. "Billy, that's horrible! How can you even think it?"

"You told me yourself how he feels about Miss Amelia," Billy explained. "What if he knew what'd happened between her and Mr. Bertie? I'd gladly knock anybody over the head if they went grabbing at my sister."

"Are you saying you think that Kell is guilty?"

"No, I'm not saying it's so. Only–"

"Only that I should consider the possibility?" Freddie shook his head. "Well, I can't! I won't! This really is too much! I refuse to listen to another word of it. Billy, will you leave me alone, please?"

Billy didn't argue, but went into the dressing room and shut the door between them.

22

It was the middle of the night when Billy woke to the soft but distinct and all-too familiar sound of Freddie whimpering in his sleep. Then Freddie cried out loud, "No!"

Billy leapt up and went into the adjoining room. Freddie wasn't awake himself, but enough moonlight came in through the windows for Billy to see that his eyes were wide open. His hands were extended, shoving to push away some unseen object. This was why he had stayed in Freddie's service after the war. He knew that his friend couldn't be left alone. What would happen if Freddie screamed in the dark and no one was there to come to his aid?

Sitting down at the edge of the bed, he captured Freddie's wrists and spoke softly but urgently to him. "Freddie, wake up. Can't you hear me?" He gave Freddie a shake. "Please, wake up!"

"Bill–?"

"Right here." Freddie's eyes were still wide and unfocused; Billy let go of his wrists and took his head between both hands, forcing Freddie to look at him.

At last, Freddie's eyes found him. "Oh, Billy," he sobbed, and his head fell forward against Billy's chest.

"Hush now." Billy put an arm around him, resting his cheek atop Freddie's head and rocking him. "There, there," he crooned like a nursery-maid comforting a frightened child. "It's all right. It's past. You're safely out of it."

"Sometimes," Freddie said, muffled against his chest, "I'm afraid I won't ever be out of it."

Billy didn't like to admit it, but he was afraid of this too.

At a knock on the door, he started guiltily, suddenly mindful that they weren't alone. There was a houseful of people around them. Leaving

Freddie, he got up to answer the door and found himself face to face with Lady Marshbourne in her dressing gown.

"Is Freddie all right?" Emily asked. "I heard him cry out." She raised a candlestick to cast some light into the darkened room behind Billy; Freddie lay curled on the bed with his head in his arms.

"He's all right, M'lady," Billy hastened to assure her. "He's just had a bad dream, remembering the war. I'll take care of him, don't you worry. I've been through this with him plenty of times and I know what to do."

For the first time since he'd entered Marsh Hall, Emily considered him. "What is your name, lad?"

"Bill Watkins, Your Ladyship."

Her expression brightened. "Why, you're the 'Billy' that Freddie used to mention so often in his letters, aren't you? You served with him at the front and pulled him out of a burning building when he was wounded."

"Yes'm, that's me," Billy murmured diffidently. "I look after Mr. Freddie now we're home again. 'Tis my work, you might say."

"Freddie isn't well, is he?" she asked in a lowered voice.

Normally, Billy's fierce sense of loyalty kept him from discussing Freddie's health with outsiders—but while Lady Marshbourne was a stranger to him, she was the nearest Freddie had to a mother. Hadn't Freddie said so often enough? If anybody had a right to know, she did.

"No, Your Ladyship," Billy told her in an equally low and confidential tone. "He's still poorly."

Emily nodded solemnly. "I was afraid of that. The poor, dear boy looked so pale and weary when he arrived yesterday, and this recent family misfortune has been so very distressing for us all. I'll leave you to care for him. If you need anything, please don't hesitate to call upon me." Other members of the family who slept nearby had come out into the hallway and were murmuring in confusion and concern; as she turned away from Freddie's door, Emily spoke to them softly, told them, "It's nothing. Only a bad dream," and shepherded them back to their rooms.

Billy shut the door and returned to Freddie. "Do you want me to stay here by you tonight?"

"Please."

Billy resumed his seat on the bed and pulled the bedclothes up to tuck Freddie in. He was prepared to sit up in vigil all night if he had to. He'd done so before.

Freddie was silent for so long that Billy began to believe he'd fallen back to sleep. Then he said, "All the time we were in France, knee-deep in mud with shells going off all around, I thought of the English countryside and my home. Marsh Hall seemed like the one place in the world where there were never any troubles. But I was wrong. There are troubles here too. In some ways, it's worse, because this is home."

"You've worn yourself out with all this running about and fretting over Cap'n Kell," Billy told him. "I was worried you would. And I didn't help you any, saying what I did about your family. I should've kept my mouth shut."

"No, Billy, you only spoke aloud what was already in my own mind. That's why I snapped and flew at you the way I did. I'm sorry. I didn't think things through. When I started to look into this, I only wanted to help Kell. I didn't consider that other Marshes might be involved. And yet, when the clues began to point toward them, I found myself looking at Marcus, Dotty, even Mellie, as possible murderers! I didn't want to have such awful thoughts about my own cousins—but I have from the first. I can't help it."

"And it's brought on one of your bad spells. Was it the same dream as before?"

"Yes, except that it's not a dream," Freddie replied. "You know that as well as I do. It's my worst memory."

Billy felt a stab of dread in his heart at these words. "I thought you couldn't remember what happened?"

"It's all in bits and pieces. Flashes come back to me. Not all of it makes sense. It is like a bad dream." Freddie lifted his head. "You've never been seriously ill, have you, Billy? Never been feverish, delirious, out of your head with pain and fear?"

"No." In fact, Billy had never been sick a day in his life.

"But that's just what it seems like. It begins quite normally. I'm in Colonel Chapman's office and we're speaking of routine matters. And then it's as if the earth opens beneath us and swallows us in flames. Fire everywhere. I feel as if the flesh is being burnt off of me and nothing's left but charred bone; but of course it wasn't as bad as that." He raised his scarred hand. "I was only burnt a little."

"That's right," said Billy. "When the roof

fell in, this big piece of wood almost landed on top of you. It just caught your hand and the side of your leg." He didn't mention that the falling roof had killed the colonel and another officer in the room. There'd been no hope of saving them, but he'd found Freddie alive. "I carried you out to the road."

"I don't remember that at all. I remember that you were crying, and I felt sorry for you. Poor Billy."

"I was afraid you'd die before help came," Billy whispered. "I was never so scared in my life. What else do you remember?" His heart was pounding as he asked the question, for Freddie was able to recall more of what had happened that day when the company headquarters had exploded. Freddie had been one of the few survivors inside. Billy, waiting outside, had made his way into the burning building, hoping against hope. His hands had shaken as he'd desperately pushed the rubble off Freddie's body. He could never forget the horror he'd felt at the amount of blood seeping through his friend's trouser leg. Yes, he'd wept over Freddie and prayed that it wasn't too late. And when he'd heard the ambulance men coming, his relief had been so great that he'd kissed his injured friend on the mouth. Surely Freddie didn't remember that? He gave no sign of it. Although Billy didn't think Freddie would mind very much if he did remember, he hoped all the same that the memory of it would remain permanently lost.

Was it his imagination, or did Freddie hesitate before he answered, "Nothing much, Bill. I'm afraid that's all there is."

•••

23

They awoke the next morning to a tap on the door. Billy had fallen asleep across the foot of Freddie's bed; his head lay pillowed on Freddie's legs. He leapt up quickly, before Freddie could realize it. There was no time to run to his own room to find his bathrobe, so he plucked up Freddie's from the post at the foot of the bed and pulled it on on his way to the door.

When he opened it, the yellow-haired maid he'd questioned the day before stood there holding a tray laden with a teapot and cup, a rack of fresh toast, and small pots of honey, butter, and jam. She smiled at him as she entered the room,

"Her Ladyship sent this up to Mr. Freddie," she announced as she let Billy take the tray from her. "She says she hopes he didn't have too bad a night."

"I'm much better, thank you." Freddie answered from under the blankets. "Please tell Aunt Emily that I'll be down soon."

The maid curtseyed and departed. Billy brought the tray to the bed and set it down across Freddie's lap. Freddie took a piece of toast to nibble on while Billy poured out some tea for him. In spite of what he'd told the maid, he looked more pale than usual and there were shadows under his eyes.

"I shouldn't have slept in so late," he said. "There's too much to do today. I have to see that Mellie talks to the police and Kell is fully cleared. I won't have finished what I set out to do until then."

"No more investigating?" Billy asked.

Freddie shook his head, and buttered another piece of toast. "It's not my business to catch this murderer, Billy, if there is such a creature. As a matter of fact, I'm beginning to think that the aunties have the right way of looking at this: If it wasn't an accident, then it must've been some wandering tramp. Not one of us."

In spite of this declaration, Billy realized that Freddie was still afraid that one of the Marshes was involved. If there was to be an arrest, then Freddie didn't want to be responsible for sending a member of his own family to prison or the gallows.

"There's something else I've been wanting to speak to you about. It's been on my mind," Freddie went on as he brushed some crumbs from his pajama top. "It concerns marriage."

Billy was surprised and somewhat alarmed by this statement. "Are you thinking of getting married? Not– not to Miss Amelia?" He couldn't help but recall how vehemently Freddie had defended his pretty cousin, nor how much time Freddie had spent in her room last night.

"No," Freddie laughed, "not to Mellie. Kell isn't the only one who regards her as a sister. There's no one I intend to marry right now. But, Billy, you used to be sweet on that barmaid at the Rose and Crown in Abbotshill."

"What if I was?" Billy replied defensively.

"You'd probably be married by now if it weren't for me. You'd make someone a wonderful husband, Billy," Freddie said as he sipped his cup of tea. "Girls like you. You've made quite a stir among the maidservants here at the Hall. Lily... and what's the name of this one?" He nodded toward the door to indicate the maid who had brought in the tray. "Effie?"

"That's right," Billy answered, blushing. "Her name's Effie."

"I saw how she smiled at you."

"What of it?" Billy wasn't certain what to make of this, but he was sure he didn't like it.

"I wouldn't like to keep you from having a normal life," Freddie told him. "I can't tell you how very glad I am to have you with me, but it isn't fair that you should spend your best years caring for an invalid." Billy let out a cry of protest, and Freddie responded swiftly, "I'm not well, Bill, and you know it as well as I do. I heard you tell Aunt Emily so last night. You would never have done that if it weren't true. My leg may have healed, but my mind still has a long way to go."

"You'll get well again," Billy insisted. "You just need to rest and not think so much about things that upset you."

"I can't avoid that. Life is full of upsetting things."

"You're in particular low spirits because of that bad turn you had last night. It's making you say things you don't mean. I don't mind looking after you, Freddie. You know I don't!'"

"I know, but you might have so much more. Old Harry Watkins has served my uncle Hill for nearly 50 years, but that hasn't prevented him from having a wife and children and a home of his own. Nor should I stop you. That's all I wanted to say."

"All right," Billy accepted this. "You've said it. Are you done with this nonsense?"

"For the moment," Freddie answered, smiling.

"Then you finish that tea and get washed and dressed. You'll feel better once you have a proper breakfast in you."

When Freddie went downstairs, he found his aunts in the dining room, chattering excitedly. Winthrop and Kellynch were there as well, the latter apparently in a state of shock.

Emily went to him as he entered the room, smiling and looking more like her usual girlish self than Freddie had seen during this visit. "How good to see you up. Are you feeling better, dear? You gave us all a very bad fright last night." She took his arm to lead him toward the others seated at the table. "Have you heard the news? Kell's no longer suspected."

"No, I hadn't heard. That's wonderful news." It looked as if his plans for the day were nullified—but Freddie didn't mind it a bit. "What happened?" he asked Winthrop. "Did Mellie talk to you?"

"Amelia came to me early this morning," his uncle confirmed. "You know about that, Freddie? The incident between her and Bertie?"

"She told me about it yesterday. I hoped she would come forward and tell you the truth."

"It can't be true," Kellynch murmured, stunned. "Not my Bertie."

"I find it hard to believe of Bertie myself," said Winthrop. "He always seemed like such a well-behaved lad—but I don't doubt Amelia's word," he added quickly, for Theresa was scowling at him. "The girl has no reason to lie. Indeed, her reluctance to speak of it 'til now proclaims the delicacy of her position."

"I wish she'd come forward sooner for Kell's sake," Emily said, "but I understand why Amelia wouldn't like to say anything so awful about a cousin."

"And Bertie engaged to her sister!" cried Celia. "Poor Bertie. He never knew when to keep his hands to himself."

"Since it looks as if the whole thing was an accident," Winthrop concluded, "I've telephoned the George and Dragon and spoken to that inspector staying there. He'll come to hear Mellie's story for himself later this morning, but he agrees that Kell is no longer a suspect in his cousin's death." He looked at his brother as if he expected Kellynch to dispute this, but Kellynch had no argument to make.

Freddie looked around the room. None of the young people except Celia, Louisa, and Marcus were present. "Where's Mellie now?"

"She and Agatha left just after they finished their breakfast," said Theresa. "She was very anxious to see her sister get away to Rose Cottage, but she promised she would return here before luncheon to see the inspector."

"Will you have some breakfast yourself, Freddie?" Emily offered.

"If you don't mind, Auntie, I'd like to go to Marshbanks right away," Freddie told her. "If I can't give Kell the good news personally, I'd like to be there to bring him home."

Freddie hastily collected Billy from the servants' hall and they were soon walking on the woodland path toward Marshbanks.

"So that's it then," said Billy. "This business

is finished?"

"As far as we are concerned, yes."

"And was it murder?"

Freddie shook his head. "I don't suppose we'll ever find out what truly happened that day beside the river. Everyone seems happy to call Bertie's death an accident. Since there's nothing to indicate otherwise, we must be satisfied with that. If the police want to go on hunting for a murderer, let them have their fun as long as Kell is safe and no other Marshes are arrested."

While they were still in the woods, they heard music coming from somewhere ahead of them. Curious to trace the source of the sound, Freddie chose a fork in the path that would bring them out at the upper end of the lane instead of near the river. They emerged from the cover of the trees in sight of Thicket Cottage. The music came from the cottage; a gramophone blared "I'll Build a Stairway to Paradise," accompanied by some loud off-key singing and bursts of laughter. The red roadster was parked in the lane outside the garden gate.

"We won't need to go all the way to Marshbanks," said Freddie. "They've come back to the cottage. They must've heard the news already." If Uncle Win had phoned Inspector Deffords, then he would likely have told them.

"Sounds like they're having a party," Billy observed. "Should we go in?"

"Yes, why not? They won't mind, and I want to see Kell." Freddie walked up the path through the untended garden. The front door of the cottage had been left open, and he went inside without knocking.

Kell and Phillip were dancing in the parlor. As they bounded back and forth across the floor, they paid no attention to where they were going, and nearly bumped into Freddie as he and Billy entered the room.

"Freddie, hello!" Kell shouted over the music and flung one arm around Freddie's neck; the other was still around Phillip's waist. "I didn't hear you come in! We're celebrating my innocence. We would've sent you an invitation, but I wanted a little time with Phil first, you understand."

He kissed Phillip's cheek, then Freddie's. When he offered to kiss Billy too, Billy drew back quickly and said, "No, thanks." But Kell was in too effusive a mood to be refused, and Billy felt the brush of that tawny mustache on his jaw anyway.

"Well, as long as you're here, join the party." Kell let go of both cousins and flopped into the nearest armchair.

Phillip plucked the gramophone needle up off the record. "Something to drink?" he offered. "There's some ginger-beer in the icebox." He went into the kitchen to get it.

Freddie sat down in the only other armchair. "It's good to see you so happy again."

"It's good to be so happy!" Kell responded cheerfully. "I haven't felt like this since the Armistice."

"Do you know why the police aren't interested in you any more?"

"New facts came to light, Hobart said, but he didn't say what they were."

"It was Mellie," Freddie told him, and noted that Kell looked very interested, but not very surprised. "She came forward and told your father that Bertie had accosted her. She didn't kill him, but she did hit him in the head with her shoe to escape."

"Is that how it happened?" Kell smiled. "Well, then, if Bertie fell into the river after that, it was only his own fault—and good riddance!"

"Kell, why didn't you tell me about Mellie?" Freddie asked. "You knew she was there, didn't you? You knew that broken earring was hers when I showed it to you."

"I knew," Kell admitted. "Mother gave her those earrings and a matching necklace as a birthday present." He blew out a puff of breath, and explained in more mollifying tones, "I didn't tell you, Freddie old thing, because I thought that if Mellie was the one to knock Bertie into the river, then she must've had a good reason for it. I wasn't eager to be hanged, but I wasn't going to put a noose around her neck either. I'm grateful she came forward at last, and I'm glad to hear she didn't kill Bertie after all."

"That was Mr. Freddie's doing," Billy informed him. "He convinced her to tell what'd happened."

"Then I'm grateful to him too." Kell grinned at Freddie. "I said you'd be a better detective than our village constable, didn't I? And I was right!"

"He would've done better if you'd told us the truth yesterday," Billy grumbled.

"I don't see how you could've worked it out more quickly," Kell retorted. "You found out about Mellie without my help. The police never got as far as that. If it were left up to them and their official inquiries, who knows how I might've ended up?"

Phillip returned from the kitchen with four

chilled bottles of ginger-beer and handed them around.

"Everything's turned out all right," Kell went on. "We won't have to fly from the country in disgrace."

"I never wanted to go," said Phillip.

"We'll go to the Hall for dinner tonight and I'll make peace with Father. I'll promise to marry... oh, whoever he likes and whomever will have me—Louisa Burke, one of Phil's sisters. How about you, Phil? You ought to have a wife too. One each. That's only fair."

"What about Mellie?" Phillip teased. "She's a nice girl, pretty too–"

"And she isn't afraid to knock a fellow over the head if he gets presumptuous! I daresay a knock in the head might do you good once in awhile, but Mellie deserves a better husband. Besides, she's had an eye on your cousin Evelyn since they were children." Kell scowled. "I'm not sorry Bertie's dead, now I know what he did to her. If I'd heard about it before, I would've given him a good shove into the river myself, just as they said I did."

Freddie glanced apologetically at Billy; so he'd been right about that.

"Perhaps it's what any brother would do in such a case," he conceded. "As a matter of fact, I wonder if Marcus actually saw Mellie running up from the river, just as Uncle Nick did—only he knew who it was and kept his mouth shut about it. He was very angry when I started to ask questions about who he'd seen in the lane that day. He wouldn't do anything to endanger either of his sisters. I wonder if he guessed what'd happened."

It occurred to Freddie that there was

another person who might have known that Bertie had assaulted Amelia on that day. Who had to know.

Suddenly, he saw that it was exactly as Billy had said: *I'd gladly knock anybody over the head if they went grabbing at my sister.* But it wasn't Kell who had claimed that vengeance, nor even Mellie's own brother Marcus. It was someone who, by striking Bertie down, was not only defending her younger sister but also taking a special revenge of her own against a faithless lover.

"Mellie went with Agatha to her cottage earlier this morning," he spoke urgently. "We've got to go and find them. I want to see Agatha."

"Whatever for?" asked Phillip.

Billy had followed Freddie's thoughts. "You think it's her? It's Miss Agatha?"

"Agatha?" Kell echoed, sitting upright. "Freddie, are you sure of that?"

"I've been wrong before," Freddie admitted, "but I don't think I am this time. Who had a better reason for wanting Bertie dead?" He rose from his chair. "I'd like to see her. I'm worried for her— for both of them. If I'm right, what do you think Agatha will do now that Mellie's told her story?"

24

Rose Cottage was only a few hundred yards down the lane from Thicket Cottage. The four young men reached it within a minute. Smoke rose in thick plumes from the chimney.

Freddie knocked insistently on the door, and was relieved when Amelia answered. "Mellie, where's your sister?" he asked. "I want to talk to her, please."

"She's sleeping," Amelia told him, her eyes flitting from face to face with curiosity and wariness. "This has been horrible for her. You saw how upset she was at the funeral yesterday. I had to get her away from the Hall."

"It was Agatha, wasn't it?" blurted Phillip. "She pushed Bertie in?"

"Did she, Mellie?" Kell asked.

"Hush. She'll hear you." Amelia opened the door to let them into the cottage and led them to the parlor. Even though it was a warm morning, a fire was blazing. As they gathered in the room, Amelia sat down before the hearth. Piles of papers tied with ribbons, open boxes, and other clutter lay on the floor, as if she'd been sorting through them when interrupted by their arrival.

Freddie crouched down beside her. "Mellie," he began in a low voice, "when you were walking by the river that day, you were coming to see your sister. When you ran from Bertie, you came directly here, didn't you?"

Amelia nodded.

"Did you tell her what he did to you?"

"I didn't need to," she answered. "Agatha could see right away that something was wrong. I was hysterical. There was mud on my dress and on my feet. My hair was flying about and what was left of that broken earring was hanging from one ear. I only had to say Bertie's name. Agatha took me inside, helped me put myself back together, gave me a cup of chamomile tea. I lay down, there–" she nodded at the rosewood settee where Phillip had taken a seat. "I must've fallen asleep, for the next thing I knew, it was afternoon. Agatha came to wake me. We went back to the Hall together.

I didn't even know Bertie was missing until later that evening, when I heard that you'd found his boat in the same spot where I'd left him."

"She went down to the river once you were asleep," said Freddie. "Bertie was still there, dazed after you'd hit him. Perhaps she confronted him, or she may simply have struck him without warning with the first weapon that came to hand."

"The boat's oars," said Kell. "They're missing. If one had blood on it, she'd only have to toss it into the water."

"Mellie, didn't you suspect her then?" Freddie asked.

"No!" she insisted. "It never occurred to me 'til I talked to you last night. Agatha was so calm, at first."

"She was quite calm when we spoke to her," said Phillip. "Remember, Kell? She was standing out in the garden pulling the deadheads off the roses when we came by. That couldn't've been long afterwards."

"She didn't begin to be upset until Bertie was found," said Amelia. "When they brought his body to Marsh Hall and the police said it was murder. I was afraid that someone would find out I'd fought with him. I'd have to say what he did to me. Agatha told me not to speak a word about it. I was to forget it'd happened. She said she'd look after me. She suggested I give away the necklace to our maid. Even last night, when I began to wonder, I didn't– I didn't want to imagine such a thing, not of my own sister! Then, when we arrived here this morning, she asked me to burn everything she had to remind her of Bertie—presents he'd given her, love notes he'd written. I found this–"

She picked up a miniature portrait of Bertie lying on the hearthrug and held it up for the boys to see; the face had been stabbed through. "The last time I was here, she was working on it to give to him. She knew about Bertie's awful reputation for chasing girls. She couldn't help it after the way he behaved with Celia last summer, but when he started keeping company with her, he promised that that was all past. She forgave him. But she couldn't forgive this."

"He told you he was going to break it off with her," said Freddie.

"He never told her," Amelia replied. "Maybe he meant to, if I'd done as he wanted. It would've broken her heart just the same. This painting is the only thing that shows how she felt." She tossed the portrait into the fire. "There." She turned to look up at them, lifting her chin defiantly. "It's gone now. There's no proof and I won't speak against her. She's my sister, no matter what she's done. When I speak to that inspector I'll say I did it—I hit Bertie harder than I meant to." Then she asked more timidly, "Will you tell?"

"I don't think we've the right to do anything," Kell said solemnly. "As far as I'm concerned, Bertie got what he deserved. It wouldn't be justice–"

A sharp bang from one of the rooms beyond cut him off and made them all jump.

"Agatha?" Amelia leapt up and went to her sister's bedroom. "She heard us!"

The room was empty and the window open. One of the casements swung free; the other had slammed itself shut. Freddie went to look out; the flowers beneath the window were crushed. "She went out this way," he told the others. "Where would she go?"

But even as he asked the question, he knew where she'd gone. They all knew. The river.

Without another word they went out of the cottage, running down the lane as fast as they could go.

As they reached the lane's end and scrambled up over the embankment, they saw her: Agatha had waded out into the shallows of the river. She hadn't troubled to lift her dress clear of the knee-high water, but was walking slowly, dragging its sodden weight, as she headed toward the deeps.

At the cries of "Agatha!" and "Stop!" behind her, she turned. Her face was white and her eyes wild with despair, but she gave her sister a smile and called out, "You won't have to lie for me, Mellie." Then she threw herself into the water. For an instant, her full skirt and long, dark hair spread out in the water, then she sank out of sight.

Amelia screamed. Freddie didn't stop to think, but slid down the grassy slope to the water's edge, and dove in. The instant he'd done it, he realized that it was foolish. Even in the midday sun, the waters of the Marshbourne were too muddy to see more than a foot beneath the surface. He could only grope blindly, hoping to catch Agatha's arm or a handful of skirt... but without luck. When he was forced to come up for air, he found he'd been caught in the undercurrent. His head barely broke the surface; he cried out once. Frantically, his arms flailed. But the current pulled him down.

After all he'd been through and survived, was it to end like this? He would drown here, so near the place where his parents had died.

The last thing he heard before the water

came up over his ears was Billy shouting his name and Kell saying, "Don't be stupid, Billy! You'll only get pulled down too." Then he went under.

There was a huge splash in the water nearby. A hand seized his coat and yanked him back toward the surface. As his face cleared the water, an arm went around his collar. "It's all right, Freddie old thing," a voice spoke against his ear. "I've got you."

Billy couldn't swim, but Kell could.

Billy had gone out into the shallows as far as he dared, dragging a large branch that had fallen from a tree overhanging the embankment. He extended it out into the water toward them; Kell caught it and they both clung to it as Billy and Phillip hauled them to safety. Freddie flopped onto the muddy bank and lay sputtering, choking, gasping for breath while Kell pounded his back to get the water out of him.

"Did you see Agatha?" he asked when he was able to speak.

"No," said Kell. "She went under even more quickly than you did, but she wasn't fighting to stay up."

They looked out over the murky waters, but saw no disturbance except for ripples made by the ordinary currents of the river. There was no sign of Agatha.

"She's gone," Amelia sobbed and sank down with her head in her hands.

25

They returned to Marsh Hall bedraggled, mud-covered, and soaked. Billy half-carried Freddie, and the others ran ahead to bring the news about Agatha. Inspector Deffords had come to interview Amelia, but the girl only flew sobbing into her mother's arms. The family's relief at seeing Kell home again quickly turned to bewilderment and sorrow at this new tragedy. Winthrop welcomed his son and, grudgingly, Phillip too, before calling for boats and sending messages to Marshbanks and the nearest farms to summon aid in searching the river.

Freddie was taken to his room, where Billy promptly got him out of his wet and muddy clothes, into a bath, then into bed. Although he was anxious to join the search for Agatha, Freddie was still coughing and wheezing from his near-drowning. While the household was in a commotion around him, he lay with a cool, damp cloth on his brow and drank hot soup and tea with honey, fed to him by Aunt Emily. She sat at his bedside and fussed over him nearly as much as Billy did.

Later in the day, he learned from Kell and Philip that the search for Agatha had been extended; the inspector had made phone calls to the constabulary in villages farther down the Marshbourne and alerted the keepers at the canal locks.

"I expect they'll find her in the rushes downstream or at one of the locks where the river is diverted around Lynn. That's where bodies usually turn up," Kell said. "That's where they found Bertie."

"Billy thinks I should go home as soon as I'm fit to travel," said Freddie, "but I believe we ought to stay until Agatha's found. There'll be another funeral to attend."

"Yes, I thought I'd stay at least that long myself," his cousin agreed.

Freddie was surprised to hear this. "Are you still thinking of leaving, Kell?"

"I thought you said you weren't going now?" asked Phillip.

"I'm not leaving England," Kell answered them both. "Why should I? The police have been called off. That inspector chap was more interested in hearing Mellie tell her story than in me. Besides, Father's relented. Finding out what Bertie was really like has come as a shock to him. He doesn't think I'm so awful anymore. He still wants me to get married, but he's given up on pushing girls at me for the time being. Louisa and Aunt Beatrice are going back to Oxford tomorrow. Chubbs was telling me that it might be best for me to get away from Marsh Hall, and I think he's right. I'd like to be somewhere else for awhile. London might be fun—that is, if you don't mind giving me a room, Freddie."

"Not at all," Freddie said. "I'll be happy to have you stay. What about your aeroplane business?"

"There's plenty of flat land here to put air-strips on, but I've a better chance of finding prospective partners in London. I'll join you once you're feeling better, old thing, and matters have been settled here. It can't be long before they find poor Agatha."

But no further news came that night.

The next morning, Freddie got up and went down to breakfast in spite of Billy's protests. The group in the dining room was morose and had nothing new to tell him.

After breakfast, he walked out to the river's edge and stood looking at the swift-flowing waters, tearing the heads off the tall flowers that grew on the embankment and tossing them in one by one to watch them catch in the current and be swept away. When he heard the sound of footsteps behind him, he turned to look up, expecting to find Billy or one of his cousins; it was Inspector Deffords.

"Have you brought news?" he asked the inspector. "Have they found her?"

Deffords shook his head. "I'm going back to Wymondham, but I wanted to talk to you before I left. I wanted to thank you for convincing Miss Amelia Marsh to tell her story. She said that you talked her into it. You did find something of hers when you waded into the reeds."

"Yes," Freddie admitted, and told the inspector about the broken earring and how he'd traced it to its owner. "I'm sorry. I should've told you about it earlier."

The inspector surprised him by saying, "We wouldn't've got to her more quickly than you did, Mr. Babington. We might never have found her at all. You had special knowledge that I didn't. There's one other thing I want to know: did she know her sister killed Bertram Marsh before she came forward?"

"Mellie didn't tell you that."

"No," the inspector admitted. "I guessed it from what she did tell me, and what she left out. She was upset over her sister and I didn't want to push her with her mother and Her Ladyship there. I decided to ask you."

Freddie saw no reason to conceal the truth

now. Deffords was no longer a danger. "Yes," he answered frankly.

"When did you know?"

"I didn't see it until it was too late. Because of my stupidity, my cousin is dead and I was nearly drowned as well. You were right, Inspector. I was a meddling amateur. Agatha would never have thrown herself into the river if it weren't for me. I should've left the investigation to you. You might never have found her out, but at least she'd still be alive."

"You don't know that," Deffords said sympathetically and offered him a cigarette. "It might've ended the same way no matter what you did. Miss Marsh's mind was unbalanced. I've seen it before. It takes cold blood to commit a murder and live with it afterwards. Her sister told me that she wanted to burn her personal possessions. That looks like she was planning to do something of the kind. That was what you were afraid of when you went to her cottage, wasn't it?"

"I thought she might harm herself, or harm Mellie. I hoped I could stop her. I wanted..." Freddie sighed and tossed the last of the flowers in his hand into the river. "I only wanted to help." He let Deffords light his cigarette before he asked, "Will this go into your report, Inspector?"

Deffords shook his head. "The case is closed. There's no one to arrest and my superiors don't want to trouble His Lordship's family without reason. We have the other girl's statement about how Bertram Marsh was killed. There's plenty of local gossip about how he chased after girls—this time, he went after the wrong one. They're calling it an accident. Death by misadventure. She'll stand by her story, won't she?"

"Amelia? Yes, more fiercely now that she's defending her sister's memory," Freddie confirmed. "The Marshes are a very close family, you know. They protect each other. Even if the rest of the family guesses at the truth, they'll hush this up. Poor Agatha went mad after the death of her fiancé. It's another tragic accident."

Kathryn L. Ramage has a B.A. and M.A. in English lit and has been writing for as long as she can remember. She lives in Maryland with two aging and chronically ill cats. As well as being the author of numerous short stories, novellas, and essays, she is the author of "Maiden in Light" and "The Wizard's Son," novels set on an alternate Earth whose history has diverged from ours somewhere during the medieval period. Both are part of an intended series of fantasy novels that mostly take place in a dukedom called the Northlands, a part of the Norman Empire that roughly covers the north-eastern U.S. Her website is at www.klr.wapshottpress.com

www.ingramcontent.com/pod-product-compliance
Lightning Source LLC
Chambersburg PA
CBHW070932130626

46555CB00001B/395